D0014716

SCHOOL of SECRETS

CARLOS'S
SCAVENGER HUNT

BY
JESSICA BRODY

PRESS

Los Angeles • New York

Copyright © 2017 Disney Enterprises, Inc.

All rights reserved. Published by Disney Press, an imprint of Disney Book Group.
No part of this book may be reproduced or transmitted in any form or by any means,
electronic or mechanical, including photocopying, recording, or by any information
storage and retrieval system, without written permission from the publisher. For
information address Disney Press, 1101 Flower Street, Glendale, California 91201.

Printed in the United States of America
First Hardcover Edition, November 2017
1 3 5 7 9 10 8 6 4 2
FAC-020093-17272

Library of Congress Control Number: 2017951336
Hardcover ISBN 978-1-368-01398-7

For more Disney Press fun, visit www.disneybooks.com
Visit DisneyDescendants.com

SUSTAINABLE Certified Sourcing
FORESTRY
INITIATIVE www.sfiprogram.org
SFI-00993

THIS LABEL APPLIES TO TEXT STOCK

GET ALL THE BOOKS IN THE SCHOOL OF SECRETS SERIES!

CJ'S TREASURE CHASE

FREDDIE'S SHADOW CARDS

ALLY'S MAD MYSTERY

LONNIE'S WARRIOR SWORD

CARLOS'S SCAVENGER HUNT

UNLEASHED

The teen had never left the island before. No one who grew up on the Isle of the Lost ever left. It was his home and his prison. But not anymore.

For the first time in his life, he was crossing over the sea. He was breaking through the barrier that separated the Isle from the great United States of Auradon. He was leaving.

And he'd never been more excited.

No more stealing. No more forcing down goblin slop for breakfast. No more of his mother's bossing him around. The teen had never been a very good villain—something his mother never failed to remind him. That was why he was so eager to leave, to start fresh and see how much he could shine in a new place.

A place like Auradon Prep.

The teen packed the last of his clothes and belongings into his duffel bag and zipped it up tight, giving it a pat. He was more than ready.

"Aren't you forgetting something?" came the ominous, screechy voice of his mother. The teen startled at the sound and turned around. He was always jumpy around his mother. She had that effect on people, especially him.

The teen unzipped his bag, studying the contents. "No. I don't think so."

His mother smiled that creepy, sinister smile of hers. It was a smile that could make even the most fearsome dogs shake in their furs. "You're forgetting this."

She reached into the sleeve of her fur coat and pulled out a small red bracelet. At least, it looked like a bracelet. But upon closer inspection, the teen noticed that it had a buckle and a silver bone-shaped tag hanging from it. Almost like . . .

"Is that a dog collar?" the teen asked, instinctively stepping back. He'd had a fear of dogs ever since he was little.

"It's not *just* a dog collar, my boy," his mother replied silkily. "It's a *magic* dog collar."

The teen frowned in confusion. Magic did not exist on the Isle of the Lost. And he'd never known his mother to use magic, even in her villainous heyday. "What does it do?"

"Whoever wears the collar gives the commands," she replied with a mischievous sneer. "Like a master with a well-trained dog, the wearer of the collar can make people obey them."

"Obey them?" the teen repeated with obvious doubt in his voice. "Really?"

"Are you calling your mother a liar?" she snapped, throwing her arms in the air. The teen cowered. He was used to his mother's short temper, but it still terrified him.

"N-no," he stammered.

His mother huffed and shoved the collar into

his hand. "Just put it in your bag. It will work in Auradon."

"But why would I need it?" the teen asked, still unsure why he was being offered the supposedly magical gift.

His mother started to laugh. It was her signature maniacal laugh—the one that rattled the boy's teeth. "Oh, foolish, foolish boy," she said. "You need it because you're weak. You're not a leader. You're a follower. And if you ever want anyone to do what you say, you're going to need help. Lots of it."

Then she laughed her evil, grating laugh again and stormed out of the room.

The teen stared at the red collar, still in his hand. The little bone-shaped tag brushed against his fingers. He clenched the soft leather of the strap as anger pulsed through him. His mother had never thought much of him. She'd never had confidence in him—which was why he had always had to find confidence in himself.

As he tossed the collar into his duffel and zipped the bag back up, he thought, *I'll prove her wrong. I'll show her that I* am *a leader. I've just been living on the wrong island.*

GOOD BOY

Hi. I'm Carlos, son of Cruella De Vil. But don't worry. I'm nothing like my mother. I love dogs. And not for making fur coats out of. It took me a little while to get over my fear of them, but now that I have, one of my best friends is a dog. His name is Dude. We met shortly after I moved to Auradon Prep.

It's one of the many things in my life that has improved since I left the Isle. Let's just say I wasn't quite cut out for life on the Isle of the Lost. It never suited me the way it used to suit Mal and Jay and even Evie. I was never very good at being evil. I've found I'm actually much better at being good. It turns out being good is not so bad. It's made me a lot more friends than I ever had on the Isle. Friends like Jane, Fairy Godmother's daughter, who happens to be one of my favorite people at Auradon Prep. She's so kind and sweet and, okay . . . very pretty. But I'm getting off topic. . . .

Making friends isn't my problem. My problem is that everyone around here seems to think of me as just Carlos, the nice villain kid (or VK, as we are known), the guy you can always rely on if you need help. But I want to be more than that. I want to be a leader. The guy who <u>makes</u> the plan, not the one who just helps out when the plan goes wrong.

All of my fellow baddies have become great leaders since we got here. Jay is tourney captain and almost always manages to lead the team to victory. Evie has basically created a fashion empire with her Evie's 4 Hearts company, and she makes huge business decisions every day. And Mal has kind of always been our unspoken leader. She's the one who came up with the plan to steal Fairy Godmother's wand. Even though that plan never actually panned out, people still look up to Mal.

And now it's my turn.

I'm determined to be a leader, too. But not just any leader. A <u>great</u> leader. A memorable leader. The kind of leader who goes down in history!

I just have to find my place to shine. . . .

TOP DOG

I hope no one notices how
fidgety I am. As my mom would
say, I'm as jumpy as a flea.

"This is the coolest school project ever!" Jane said,
sitting down in one of the large armchairs in the
Mad for Tea tea shop and pulling her notebook
out of her bag. "I can't believe they're letting us
design an actual app!"

"It is quite a fun idea," Ally agreed in her
posh English accent. Ally was the daughter of
Wonderland's Alice, and her family owned the
tea shop. She had invited Jane, Carlos, Freddie,

and Audrey to have tea on Friday afternoon while they discussed the group project they'd just been assigned in their Safety Rules for the Internet class.

Carlos was excited about the project, too, but he was also nervous. The teacher had divided the class into groups of five and told them that each group had to not only design an app but choose a project manager—someone who would lead the rest of the group and keep everyone organized and on task. Plus, that person would be the one to present the app to the entire class the next week.

Carlos had always wanted to design his own app. And he *knew* the project was just the kind of thing he'd been looking for. He could totally be the project manager. He *should* be the project manager. After all, he knew the most about technology. He just needed to figure out a way to convince the rest of his group that they should choose him.

Ally poured Carlos a cup of tea and flashed him a smile. He smiled back, but it felt forced. Should he just come right out and say it? Like "I think I should be project manager." Or should he lead with something more subtle? Like "So, what was that thing the teacher said about choosing a project manager?"

"What kind of app do you think we should create?" Jane asked, her eyes twinkling. Carlos loved when Jane's eyes twinkled like that.

"Perhaps some kind of tea party app!" Ally suggested. "It helps you plan your own tea party."

"Or," Jane said, "what about an app that organizes all of your school schedules?"

"Hmmm," Audrey said, clearly not liking either of those ideas. "I think we should build a princess makeover app. You upload a picture of yourself and the app turns you into a princess!"

"No," Freddie said immediately.

"And why not?" Audrey asked, crossing her arms over her chest.

"Because not everyone wants to be a princess," Freddie snapped back.

"Well, what do *you* suggest?" Audrey asked. "An app that turns people into frogs?"

11

Freddie nodded, clearly liking that idea. "Not bad."

"I was kidding!" Audrey said grumpily. "We are so not building an app that turns people into frogs!"

"And what is wrong with frogs?" Freddie asked defensively.

See? Carlos thought. *This is exactly why I need to be project manager. They're already arguing over what kind of app to build.*

"We should vote," Jane said diplomatically, and Carlos mentally kicked himself for not having thought of that first. That was an excellent idea— the kind of idea a good leader came up with.

"Good idea, Jane," Audrey said. "All in favor of my princess app?"

Audrey was the only one who raised her hand.

"All in favor of my tea party app?" Ally asked, and raised her hand. She was also the only one.

"All in favor of my school schedule app?" Jane said, but it was becoming apparent that everyone was voting for her own idea.

"This isn't working," Audrey complained.

Carlos's leg began to bounce anxiously. He should speak up. He should point out that they should choose a project manager *before* they decided what the app should be.

"Carlos, you're spilling your tea," Ally complained.

Carlos blinked and glanced down at the teacup on the coffee table in front of him. His knee's bouncing had been rattling the cup, and now tea was sloshing all over the saucer. "Sorry," he muttered.

"What do *you* think, Carlos?" Jane asked, flashing him a warm smile that made Carlos's stomach do a flip.

"Um," Carlos said, knowing this was his chance. It was now or never. He had to take it. "I think before we decide what app to build, we should decide who the project manager is."

Ally grinned. "Oh, yes! Brilliant idea, Carlos! Well done. Of course!"

Carlos felt incredibly proud of himself. He was

acting like a project manager already. Taking command of the situation. Setting the team on track. He knew he could lead people. He just knew it.

"And I think—" Carlos began, ready to nominate himself for the role, when suddenly Audrey interrupted him.

"Jane! You should definitely be the project manager," Audrey said.

"Oh, yes," Ally immediately chimed in. "I absolutely agree."

"Just as long as it's not me," Freddie said.

"Really?" Jane said, seeming uncertain. "You want *me* to be project manager?"

"Of course," Audrey said. "You were the one who had that amazing internship with Carina Potts last summer."

Carlos felt a swell of disappointment. That was true. The past summer, Jane *had* done an internship with Carina Potts, the daughter of Mrs. Potts and the most famous party planner in all of Auradon. That definitely made Jane a good candidate for project manager, but Carlos still really wanted it.

"Yes," Jane said, "but that didn't really give me any experience with apps."

"Doesn't matter," Audrey said. "Anyone who interns with the almighty Carina Potts has to do great work under pressure."

"Yeah, she only hires the best," Ally agreed.

Jane glanced down at her lap, looking uncomfortable, like she was desperate to change the subject. "I don't know about that. Doesn't anyone else want to do it?"

"Actually," Carlos said, "I was thinking maybe *I* could do it."

All four girls stared at him, like he was speaking another language. Then Audrey decidedly shook her head. "Carlos, you can't be project manager. You need to be in charge of all the tech stuff. The programming. You're the best there is. And we need your help."

There it was: that word Carlos was beginning to despise.

Help.

He was always the helper. Always the support

staff. Just once he wanted someone to see him as a leader, not a helper. The commander, not the soldier.

Carlos opened his mouth to speak, but once again, Audrey cut him off. "Jane is the most obvious choice for the project manager. She's the most organized. She'll keep us on track."

And before anyone—including Carlos or Jane—could argue, Audrey said, "All in favor of Jane being our project manager?"

Audrey, Freddie, and Ally raised their hands. Then all four girls looked at Carlos, and Carlos's shoulders sagged. He slowly lifted his hand into the air.

Audrey clapped once. "Then it's settled. Jane is the group leader."

RUNT OF THE LITTER

For once I want to be seen by my
friends as a leader—not just the
guy you come to when you need
help fixing your smartphone.

Later that night, at dinner, Carlos thought about what had happened in the tea shop. How everyone had immediately thought of Jane when it came time to pick a project manager. No one had even taken his suggestion seriously. Sure, he was good at all that tech stuff, and he loved doing it, but he could be good at the leadership stuff, too!

Back on the Isle it had been the same. He was

always the sidekick, never the chief villain. And when he'd come to Auradon with Evie, Mal, and Jay, and they were tasked with stealing the wand, even *then* Carlos was just the helper. He got the alarms at the Museum of Cultural History turned off so they wouldn't get caught. The team needed him when they got into trouble. That was the problem. They never looked to him to lead them away from trouble in the first place.

Carlos wondered what it was about him that made people fail to see his leadership qualities. He could be trusted to run things. He could come up with a solid plan. He could lead a team to victory. He just needed his shot.

Carlos tried to join the conversation at dinner. He was seated at a table with Mal, Evie, Jay, Lonnie, Ally, Audrey, Freddie, and Jane. They were playing the "Most Likely to" game. It was something that had sprung up recently at Auradon Prep and had become popular among the students. Normally Carlos enjoyed playing. But that day he couldn't focus. His mind kept drifting back to the tea shop.

"Most likely to own a cupcake shop?" Audrey said, starting a new round of the game.

"Ally," Jane immediately replied. "She makes the best scones in the world." Everyone nodded their agreement.

"Most likely to smuggle a pet dragon into their dorm room?" Ally asked, and the whole group immediately turned and pointed at Mal.

"Hey! My mother is not a pet," Mal said jokingly.

Everyone laughed.

"Oh, I've got one," Lonnie said. "Most likely to end up on the cover of a fashion magazine?"

"Evie," Mal replied immediately.

Evie tilted her head tenderly toward Mal. "Awww, thanks, bestie."

"No problem."

"Hello?" Audrey said, clearly offended. "What about me? I could be on the cover of a fashion magazine! A *princess* fashion magazine."

"Absolutely," Mal said, flashing Audrey a fake smile. Then she quickly asked a new question before Audrey could speak again. "Most likely to win a chess championship?"

Jay guffawed. "That's easy. Me."

Mal shot him a doubtful look. "Why you?"

Jay brushed imaginary dust off his shirt. "I'm the best at sports."

"Chess isn't a sport," Evie pointed out.

"Doesn't matter," Jay said. "If the word 'champion' is in the title, it's mine."

"I don't think so," Audrey said. "If anyone is going to win a chess championship, it's Jane. She's got the most analytical brain of us all."

Jay opened his mouth to argue, but Evie quickly interrupted with another question. "Most likely to drop their phone in the Enchanted Lake?"

"Chad!" the entire table called out at once.

Chad Charming looked up curiously from the next table. "What?"

"Nothing!" Evie called out. Then she leaned in conspiratorially and added, "He'd probably drop it in because he was so distracted staring at his own reflection."

Everyone at the table broke out into hoots of laughter—everyone except Carlos, that is. He was still lost in his own thoughts.

"Most likely to lead an army into battle?" Mal said.

Carlos perked up at that one, hoping someone might throw out his name. But they all immediately turned to Lonnie. Of course, her mother was Mulan, the great warrior. She was definitely the obvious choice.

"Most likely to become a sidekick?"

"Carlos!" the group shouted at once, and Carlos felt his shoulders slouch with disappointment.

"Really? 'Cause I see myself much more as the hero type." Carlos tried to hide the hurt in his voice.

But Jane must have heard it anyway, because she instantly tried to make him feel better. "Being a sidekick is not bad. Sidekicks are often the most important characters in a story. The heroes can't succeed without them."

"Exactly," Audrey added. "Just think about my

mother. She never would have met my father if it weren't for her meddling forest friends, stealing dad's cape and boots."

"Great," Carlos muttered under his breath. "Now they're comparing me with a bunch of rabbits and squirrels."

"What?" Jane asked, tilting her head toward Carlos.

"Nothing," he mumbled.

"Oh, I got one!" Jay said. "Most likely to—"

But he never got the chance to finish his question, because just then, the loudest bell Carlos had ever heard started to chime across the entire campus of Auradon Prep, and the very next moment, almost all the people in the banquet hall let out simultaneous screams.

PAVLOVIAN RESPONSE

Why did that bell terrify
me—and make everyone else
shout in excitement?

When Carlos heard the screams, his first reaction was to duck under the table and take cover—which, of course, was ridiculous. This was Auradon, not the Isle of the Lost. Nothing bad ever happened here. But apparently, his Isle impulses hadn't yet worn off.

Carlos chastised himself for his reaction. It reminded him of that embarrassing first day at Auradon Prep, when he saw the statue in front of the school morph from man to beast and he literally leapt into Jay's arms in fear.

Maybe this is the reason no one around here sees you as a leader, Carlos thought as he climbed out from under the table and brushed off his black-and-white leather pants. *Because you keep doing stuff like that.*

But why was everyone still screaming as though the school was being invaded by pirates?

The moment he stood up, Carlos realized that his classmates weren't all screaming in fear or panic; they were screaming with excitement.

Well, everyone except Carlos's fellow VKs—Mal, Evie, Freddie, and Jay. They were staring at each other, looking about as confused as Carlos felt. Meanwhile, the AKs (Auradon kids) were all out of their seats, jumping up and down and high-fiving each other.

"What did we miss?" Evie asked.

Mal shrugged. "I have no idea. They're acting like they just announced a royal ball or something."

Jay groaned. "Another one? Does it sometimes

feel like all these people do around here is have parties and balls?"

Carlos glanced at Jane, who was also out of her seat, bouncing up and down on her toes like a cheerleader at a tourney match. "What's going on?" he called to her.

Jane looked at him in shock, like she couldn't believe he was even asking that. "It's the annual Auradon Prep Scavenger Hunt!" she cried ecstatically. "No one ever knows exactly when it will happen—my mother likes it to be a surprise—but those bells mean it's starting this weekend!"

Carlos looked to Jay for an explanation. "The what?"

Jay shook his head. "I have no idea. They have some pretty strange traditions around here."

Carlos was about to ask Jane what this mysterious annual Auradon Prep Scavenger Hunt was when suddenly the room got very quiet and everyone turned toward the front of the banquet hall in anticipation. Carlos stood on his chair in an attempt to peer over all the heads, and that was when he saw that Headmistress Fairy Godmother had just entered the room. Her hands were held majestically in the air, like she was about to cast a spell on everyone. And in a way, she already had. The raucous noise that had caused Carlos to jump out of his seat and dive for cover had completely died down, and now everyone was staring intently at her, waiting for her to speak.

"Students! Students!" Fairy Godmother began in her usual lilting voice. "The time has finally come. The annual Auradon Prep Scavenger Hunt is upon us!"

The crowd burst into wild cheers and applause again. That is, until Fairy Godmother silenced them with another raise of her hands. Carlos glanced around at his classmates in total awe. He'd never seen them that attentive before. Whatever this scavenger hunt thing was, people were taking it *very* seriously. You would have thought Fairy Godmother was about to announce the next king and queen of Auradon.

"For those of you who are *new* to us this year,"

Fairy Godmother said with a friendly wink toward Carlos, Jay, Evie, Freddie, and Mal, "allow me to explain. As always, the school will be divided into teams of three. Each scavenger hunt team will be assigned a captain—chosen by me, of course—and that captain shall lead their team through the city of Auradon on a great quest. Team assignments and captains will be announced tomorrow on the school bulletin board. Scavenger hunt lists will be distributed via text shortly after. Each item on the list is assigned a point value based on its level of difficulty. The team to collect the most points by tomorrow at three p.m. earns the title of this year's champions!"

Carlos could already feel himself getting excited. And it wasn't just because the enthusiasm in the room was contagious. It was because Fairy Godmother had used three magic words that had especially piqued Carlos's interest: *quest, champions,* and *captain.*

"See you tomorrow morning!" Fairy Godmother said, and then strode gracefully out of the hall. The moment she disappeared, the eager chatter started up again. Everyone was talking about the hunt.

"Isn't it exciting?" Jane whispered to Carlos.

He nodded. "Definitely. I've never seen the school this worked up about something before. Not even for a tourney game. Or a party!"

Jane nodded sagely. "The annual Auradon Prep Scavenger Hunt is the biggest competition of the year."

Jay stuck his head between Carlos and Jane. "Did someone say 'competition'?"

Carlos rolled his eyes and shoved Jay's head back. "Go away."

Jane continued her explanation. "Everyone around here gets *super* into it, because the stakes are so high."

"What *are* the stakes?" Carlos asked, and Jane's eyes instantly lit up, like she was about to share with him the secrets of the universe.

"C'mon!" she squealed. "I'll show you." Then

Jane grabbed Carlos's hand, causing Carlos's face to warm like an oven.

Carlos allowed Jane to lead him to a small courtyard just off the dorms. He'd seen that courtyard before. He'd walked through it countless times on the way to classes, but he didn't understand why Jane had brought him there.

It was just a normal courtyard, with a few trees, some park benches, and tables for students to study at. He didn't understand how *that* had anything to do with a scavenger hunt.

"Not only does the winning team of the annual Auradon Prep Scavenger Hunt get epic bragging rights," Jane began. "They also get *this*." She dropped Carlos's hand and spread her arms out wide.

Carlos glanced around curiously, a scowl of confusion on his face. "A courtyard?" he asked.

Jane smiled. She had a warm, gentle smile, just like her mother. "No, silly. Look down."

Carlos looked down and noticed the courtyard

was paved with hundreds of diamond-shaped stones. On each stone, three names were engraved. Carlos had noticed the stones and the names before, but he had never thought much of them. He had always assumed they were the names of some people who were important to the school. He had never even bothered to read the names very carefully.

He bent down to study the stone he was currently standing on. It read:

HOLLISTER (TC)

SUZIE (TM)

ALIA (TM)

Carlos looked at Jane, his eyebrows pinched together. "I don't get it. What does it mean?"

She walked over and bent down next to him. She ran her fingertip over the letters carved into the stone. "These are the names of one of the winning teams. Hollister was the team captain—or

TC for short—and Suzie and Alia were the team members, or TMs."

Jane stood up and gestured to all the stones in the courtyard. There were *lots*. "These are all winners of the annual Auradon Prep Scavenger Hunt. The champions will have their names here forever. Like a permanent part of the school. A legacy. It's such an honor."

Carlos glanced around the empty courtyard, taking note of the stones that hadn't yet been engraved. He walked to one and bent down, then ran his hand over the smooth blank cement. He could almost *see* his name etched into the surface. He could almost taste the victory.

If his name was carved into one of those stones with the letters *TC* next to it, then no would ever doubt his leadership skills again. *Everyone*, from then until the end of time, would know that Carlos De Vil had led a team to victory.

ALPHA DOG

I know what I have to do. This is my big shot. My chance to prove once and for all that I am not destined to be a sidekick. I am destined to be a leader. A hero. A winner!

Carlos paced the length of his dorm room. Back and forth. Back and forth. His roommate, Jay, was at the gym, lifting weights. Carlos was alone—alone with his thoughts.

And Dude.

"Woof!" Dude barked. He was clearly getting bored with all the pacing.

"Shhh," Carlos commanded.

Dude groaned and curled up on the bed. Carlos could almost swear he saw Dude roll his eyes.

"This is serious," Carlos explained to his scruffy brown dog. "I need to figure out a way to *ensure* that Fairy Godmother chooses me as a team captain for the scavenger hunt tomorrow. This might be my one and only chance to prove to everyone that I'm a leader!"

"Woof!" Dude replied.

Carlos smiled at the dog. "Thanks, buddy. I know *you* think of me as a leader. But what about Fairy Godmother? If she doesn't think of me that way, then I can kiss my chances of becoming a team captain good-bye."

Dude sighed and rested his head on his paws. Carlos scratched him between the ears. Carlos was running out of ideas. He'd already asked Jane if maybe she could talk to her mother and try to convince Fairy Godmother to pick Carlos as a captain, but Jane had adamantly shaken her head.

"Sorry," Jane had replied. "My mother doesn't let *anyone* tell her what to do. Especially when it comes to something as serious and competitive as the annual Auradon Prep Scavenger Hunt."

So that option was out. But Carlos was getting desperate. And he was running out of time. The teams were going to be announced the next morning, and it was already eight o'clock at night. Carlos didn't want to leave this to chance. What if Fairy Godmother didn't see him as a leader, either? What if she saw him the way everyone else at the school seemed to see him: as just the nice guy who helped everyone out?

Carlos wondered if he should try to talk to Fairy Godmother himself, appeal to her, put his best foot forward. Maybe if he went to her office and tried to convince her of his leadership skills, she might—

"Woof!" Dude interrupted, jumping up from the bed and running to the door. "Woof! Woof! Woof!"

Carlos got up and opened the door. Usually

when Dude barked at the door, it meant someone was coming, but no one was there.

"Woof! Woof! Woof!" Dude continued to bark.

"What's the matter with you?" Carlos asked. "There's no one there."

"Woof! Woof! Woof!" came Dude's response.

"Dude," Carlos complained. "Stop."

"Woof! Woof! Woo—"

"Sit!" Carlos commanded, and Dude dutifully stopped barking and sat down on the floor. Carlos smiled. "Good boy." Then Carlos chuckled and sat down next to his dog. "Sometimes it feels like you're the only one around here who really takes me seriously."

Dude looked up at Carlos and seemed almost to smile.

"Roll over!" Carlos said.

Dude rolled over, and Carlos rubbed his belly and sighed. "If only everyone else around here listened to me like you do."

As soon as the words were out of his mouth, Carlos was struck with a strange memory—a memory from the Isle of the Lost. It was kind of hazy and muddled, like most of his memories from the Isle. He'd tried to block all those out a long time ago.

But now he suddenly saw his mother's face, heard his mother's voice.

If you ever want anyone to do what you say, you're going to need help. . . .

Then he heard his mother's loud cackle, and Carlos flinched. The memory of that laugh still terrified him.

But it did give Carlos an idea.

He jumped up from the floor and ran to his closet. He pulled down the giant duffel bag he'd used to pack all his things when he first came from the Isle.

He knew that memory he'd just had. He knew it was from the day he came to Auradon. He had been packing up all his things and his mother had come into his room and . . .

Whoever wears the collar gives the commands. . . .

Carlos stuck his hand into the giant duffel,

feeling around until his fingers brushed against something soft and worn and leathery. He had never even unpacked it. It fact, he'd forgotten all about it until that moment, mostly because he hadn't taken it seriously. He'd never thought it would actually work. His mother had been getting more and more delusional, and she oftentimes stretched the truth.

But now, as Carlos pulled his hand out of the duffel to reveal the small red dog collar with the bone-shaped metal tag dangling from it, he had to wonder.

Could his mother be right?

Was the little dog collar really magic?

RED-COLLAR JOB

Obviously I need to test this puppy out.

Carlos slipped the collar on like a wristband. Then he opened his dorm room door again and poked his head into the hallway. He looked left and right, but the hallway was still empty. Then, just before he was about to close the door, Carlos heard footsteps. His head whipped to the left, and he saw Chad Charming strolling down the hall toward his own dorm room.

"Chad!" Carlos called out. "Wait!"

Chad stopped mid-step, like he'd been physically frozen. Carlos studied Chad. Then he glanced down curiously at the collar around his wrist. Was Chad truly following his command? Or was that just a coincidence?

Carlos bit his lip. "Chad, come here!"

Chad immediately turned and ran toward Carlos, as eager and obedient as Dude when he was ready for his morning walk.

Weird, Carlos thought, feeling a tingle of anticipation run through him. But he told himself not to get too excited. Chad could easily just have been being nice, or maybe Chad was wondering what Carlos had to say.

"What's up, Carlos?" Chad asked, his eyes wide, like he was hanging on Carlos's next word.

"Um," Carlos said, trying to think of a good command. He needed to think of something Chad wouldn't normally agree to do. Something a *prince* would never do. Carlos's lips curved into a wicked grin.

"Chad, shine my shoe!"

Chad looked at him strangely for a moment, as though he was questioning Carlos's sanity. Carlos felt his heart sink. Of course it didn't work. Of course his mother didn't have a magic dog collar. His mother had probably been playing a prank on him, hoping he'd fall for it so she could laugh her evil, maniacal laugh at him. Carlos felt foolish for having believed it even for a second.

But then Chad tilted his head to the side and asked, "Which one?"

Carlos blinked. "Huh?"

"Which shoe?" Chad said, clarifying his question.

Was Chad being serious, or was he just joking around? There was only one way to find out.

"Um . . . the left one," Carlos replied.

And then, in total disbelief and utter shock, Carlos watched Chad pull a handkerchief from his pocket, drop to the floor, and start to shine Carlos's left shoe. Carlos jumped back. "Stop! Stop! I'm kidding! You don't have to shine my shoe."

Chad remained on the floor, glancing up at Carlos as though waiting for him to tell him what to do next. Carlos subtly slipped the dog collar from his wrist, and the moment he did, Chad leapt up from the floor, brushing himself off.

"Uh, what was I doing on the floor?" he asked, looking confused, like he'd just come out of a trance.

Carlos pretended to be clueless. "I have no idea."

"That was weird," Chad said.

"It certainly was," Carlos agreed, and then went back into his room and closed the door. As soon as he was alone again, he stared down at the dog collar in his hand.

It looked so boring and simple. A red dog collar with a bone-shaped metal tag. Nothing special. It didn't glow or sparkle or shimmer. In fact, it looked old and worn. Carlos wondered where his mother had acquired it and how it had become magical.

But it didn't much matter, did it? All that mattered was that it worked.

Carlos's face broke into a wide grin as he slipped the collar back onto his wrist, hid it under the sleeve of his black, white, and red leather jacket, and strode purposefully toward the door.

"Woof!" Dude said.

"No, you stay here," Carlos replied, feeling more confident than he'd felt in a long time. "I have an appointment with a fairy godmother. And just like Cinderella, I'm hoping she'll make all my dreams come true."

ITCHING TO
BE CAPTAIN

I will only use the dog collar to get
myself named team captain. I will not
use it to win the scavenger hunt.

As he walked toward the headmistress's office,
Carlos made a vow to himself that he would
not cheat at the competition; if he did, the win
wouldn't count. At least, not in his eyes. It would
feel empty. Void of any meaning. And he didn't
want to win that way. He knew that if he got a
chance to lead a team, he could win the game himself. He just needed help getting that chance. This
wasn't cheating. This was simply a little leg up.

When he reached Fairy Godmother's office, he saw she was leaving. She held a large brown leather satchel in her hand. Carlos ran to catch up to her. "Fairy Godmother! Wait up!"

Fairy Godmother obediently stopped and turned. Carlos gently touched the dog collar under his jacket sleeve and tried to hide the triumphant smile on his face. It was working already!

"Good evening, Carlos," Fairy Godmother said, smiling her tender smile. "I was just leaving. Walk with me."

The headmistress began to stroll along the beautifully landscaped walkways of the Auradon Prep campus, her sensible heels click-clacking on the pavement. "What can I do for you?" she asked.

Carlos opened his mouth to speak but suddenly felt nervous. Was he really about to *command* the headmistress of the school? Was he really going to give Fairy Godmother—*the* Fairy Godmother—a direct order? He'd never given a direct order to someone of her authority. He worried he wouldn't be able to do it. He worried he wouldn't be able to ⋅physically form the words.

Come on! Carlos scolded himself. *This is what being a leader is all about. Giving commands. Taking charge. If you can't give a simple order now, how do you expect to lead an entire team to victory tomorrow?*

His pep talk seemed to work. He stood up a bit straighter and said, "Fairy Godmother, I'd like to talk to you about the scavenger hunt."

Even the headmistress seemed to get a little giddy at the mention of the big competition. She perked up and let out a tinkling little laugh. "Oh, yes! The scavenger hunt! Are you excited? I'm excited." She lifted the brown satchel in her hand and gave it a dainty little *pat-pat*. "I've got the teams and final item list right here. This year is going to be the most epic hunt ever, if I do say so myself."

Carlos knew it was now or never.

"Yes, right," he said, taking a deep breath to

steady his nerves. "So, I would like to be captain of one of the teams."

Fairy Godmother stopped walking. She turned to Carlos with a look of disappointment and made a *tsk* sound with her tongue. "Now, Carlos, I know you're still new to the school and haven't yet competed in this hunt, but you should know that a lot of people want to be captain. If I granted everyone's wish to be captain, we'd have more captains than teams! Therefore, I don't take any requests from students. I make these decisions entirely on my own."

Not this time, Carlos thought nervously.

He swallowed hard. He couldn't believe what he was about to do, but he needed his shot. He needed his chance. He couldn't let this opportunity pass him by.

Carlos puffed up his chest, trying to appear bigger than he actually was, and said, "Fairy Godmother, you *will* make me a team captain."

For a long time, the headmistress just stood there, gaping at Carlos like she didn't even recognize him. And he supposed that made sense. He didn't *feel* like himself. He felt like a completely different person. A more confident person. A person who gave orders and got results. He felt like a captain.

In fact, he was so confident that his command had worked, he didn't even wait around for Fairy Godmother to respond. He just nodded, said "Good night" in a stern voice, and turned back toward the dorms.

The whole way back he couldn't keep a silly grin off his face.

As he returned to his dorm room and slipped the magic dog collar back into his duffel bag, he whispered his new title aloud: "Carlos De Vil, team captain."

He really liked the sound of that.

LET SLEEPING DOGS LIE

Unless they've got big plans. And I've got to get to the banquet hall pronto.

Everyone was up bright and early the next morning, milling around the bulletin board in the banquet hall. Carlos was too nervous to eat his breakfast. All the confidence he'd had walking home the night before was suddenly gone. What if dog collars didn't work on fairy godmothers? What if the dog collar had only enough magic in it for one person and he'd wasted it all on Chad Charming? What if the teams got posted and his name wasn't listed as captain?

When Fairy Godmother, holding her brown leather satchel, appeared inside the banquet hall, Carlos felt as though his heart leapt into his throat. Once again the banquet hall fell silent as Fairy Godmother approached the bulletin board. When she opened the satchel and pulled out a large paper scroll—the master team roster—it was as though the entire banquet hall had stopped breathing.

"I hope we're on the same team," Jane said to him, grabbing his arm and squeezing it. Carlos's throat went dry. He tried to swallow, but feeling Jane's hand on his arm made it difficult.

Fairy Godmother ceremoniously unfurled the giant scroll and pinned it to the board. Then, with a flourish and a bow, she said, "Let the annual Auradon Prep Scavenger Hunt begin! May the best team win!"

The moment she stepped away from the bulletin board, there was a mad rush across the banquet hall. Students were running and pushing and tripping over each other. Carlos thought the whole thing was very *un*-Auradon-like. It was as though that competition was the one day a year when the AKs acted like . . . well, *VKs*. Auradon kids were normally so polite and well-behaved and courteous. But not that day. Not with scavenger hunt glory on the line. Jane had been right. The stakes were *high*, and it showed.

Carlos's heart was pounding as he slowly maneuvered through the crowd toward the bulletin board. He heard people shouting with excitement upon finding their names on the roster Fairy Godmother had pinned to the board.

"*Yes!*" Jay shouted, pumping his fist. "Team captain! Of *course.*" He turned to Lonnie and Mal. "You two are with me, and we're going to rock this." He put his hand in the air, and the two girls immediately high-fived him.

Well, at least I'm not taking orders from him, Carlos thought, feeling relieved. Jay was one of his best friends, but sometimes he could be a little full of himself.

Carlos crept closer to the board, squinting at the blur of names on the long scroll.

"Oh, snap!" Jordan, the Genie's daughter, called out as she stepped away from the board. She turned to King Ben and Chad Charming. "Looks like *you* two royal highnesses are under *my* rule this weekend. Come on. Follow me. We need to start talking strategy." Ben and Chad exchanged uneasy glances but then dutifully followed Jordan to a nearby table.

The suspense was killing Carlos. He tried to elbow his way through the crowd, but there were still too many people blocking his view of the scroll.

"*What?*" he heard Audrey screech. He stood on his tiptoes to see Audrey scowling with her hands on her hips. "There's no way I'm taking directions from *her.*"

Then Carlos heard an evil laugh and saw Freddie staring at the roster. "Looks like you don't have a choice," Freddie said gleefully. "Read 'em and weep. For the next five hours, you and Ally have to do what I say."

Audrey's eyes got wide, like she was about to cry. "Fairy Godmother!" she wailed. "This is so not fair. You have to switch me."

But Fairy Godmother shook her head, looking mighty pleased with her selections. "Sorry, Audrey. You know the rules. The team roster is final. No changes."

Audrey stomped away from the board, leaving a tiny crevice of space. Carlos darted forward to fill it. He let out a sigh. He'd finally made it to the bulletin board! He cast his eyes upward, taking in the long list of teams. There were so many!

He scanned the scroll, searching for his name. But the farther he moved down the paper, the more convinced he became that he wasn't even *on* the roster.

Had Fairy Godmother forgotten to include him? Was he being disqualified for trying to force her to make him a team captain?

Carlos heard a soft squeal, and he turned to see Jane, who had snuck up to the board as well. Her eyes lit up like fireworks as she stared at the very last team on the scroll.

Carlos felt his heart sink. Of course she would get chosen. She had gotten chosen as the project manager for their class project, and now she had been chosen as their team captain for the scavenger hunt. No one had a problem seeing Jane as a leader. Not Carina Potts, and obviously not Fairy Godmother, either. She was organized and efficient and on top of everything. She was a natural.

Carlos sighed and was about to congratulate Jane. After all, he didn't want to be a sore loser, and Jane deserved the role just as much as he did.

But as he opened his mouth to speak, Jane blurted out, "Congrats, Carlos! I knew you could do it!"

Carlos frowned. *Congrats? Why is* she *congratulating* me?

But then Carlos noticed Jane was pointing at

something on the bulletin board. He crouched down and squinted at the scroll. And then he saw it. That was when Carlos De Vil finally went from sidekick to superhero.

TEAM CAPTAIN: CARLOS
TEAM MEMBERS: JANE AND EVIE

STAY WHAT?

It worked! The dog collar worked!

Carlos had given the command and Fairy Godmother had followed it. And now he was going to lead a team! He rather liked his team, too. Jane and Evie were some of his favorite people. There was no way they were going to lose this. With Carlos's leadership skills and Jane's organizational skills and Evie's . . .

Wait a minute. Where is *Evie?* Carlos thought as he and Jane took seats at one of the dining tables to await the distribution of the scavenger hunt list. Carlos didn't remember seeing her during the mad rush to the bulletin board. In fact, he wasn't sure he'd seen her at all during breakfast.

"Have you seen Evie?" Carlos asked Jane.

"Oh," Jane said. "Yeah, she said she was going to be late to breakfast because she had to finish up something important in her dorm room."

Something important? What could be more important than the annual Auradon Prep Scavenger Hunt? Does she not understand what the stakes are?

Carlos told himself to brush it off. *She'll be here. She's probably finishing up some homework so she can then devote* all *of her time to the hunt.* Carlos certainly couldn't blame her for that.

He shrugged. "Okay. Just as long as she's here before we get the—"

Carlos was about to say *item list*, but just then, every single phone in the banquet hall started to beep, startling him. There were so many phones beeping at once that it sounded like an electronic cricket symphony. Curious, Carlos looked at the message that had just arrived on his phone—and apparently on everyone else's phone as well. He saw the subject line, and his adrenaline kicked up about thirty notches.

The Official List for the Annual Auradon Prep Scavenger Hunt

"This is it!" Jane cried, staring at the screen of her own phone. "It's starting!"

No, Carlos thought, craning his neck to see above all the people milling about the banquet hall. *It can't start yet. Evie isn't even here!*

Carlos read the first few lines of the message.

Welcome, team members and team captains! The hunt is now afoot! Remember, items on this list are assigned point values according to level of difficulty. You must take a time-stamped photograph of each item for it to count. The team with the most points by 3:00 p.m. today will win the title of Auradon Prep Scavenger Hunt Champions! There is only one rule: you MUST stick together as a team.

Carlos caught just a glimpse of the first item on the list peeking out from the bottom of his phone screen, but he wouldn't let himself look at it. And he told Jane not to, either. Not until they were all there. He wanted to do this as a team. So instead, Carlos composed a new message and sent it to Evie.

Where are you? Hunt is starting!

Her response came almost immediately, as though she was already staring at her phone when Carlos's message arrived.

So sorry! On my way down now!

Carlos was desperate to look at the items, but he forced himself not to, keeping his gaze trained on the door as they waited for Evie. But the longer they waited, the more he heard *other* teams already buzzing about the list, and it was really starting to make him antsy.

"Oh, seriously, did you see number two?" Freddie asked her team. "So easy."

"Yeah, but what about number six?" Ally replied, sounding concerned. "That's practically impassable!"

"I think you mean *impossible*," Audrey said, clearly still sour from her team assignment.

"No, I mean impassable," Ally replied.

"Okay, boys," Jordan was saying to Ben and Chad. "We're tackling number eleven first."

"What? But that one seems so hard," Chad argued. "Shouldn't we start with something easier?"

"Don't argue with your captain," Jordan scolded in a teasing voice. "C'mon, Your Majesties, let's go."

As teams started to file out of the room and the banquet hall became emptier and emptier, Carlos was about to boil over with anticipation. There was still no sign of Evie, but Carlos couldn't take the suspense any longer. He knew he couldn't leave without her. The rule was they had to stick together. But at least he could start thinking about how to acquire some of the items.

"Okay, we can't wait anymore," he told Jane. "Let's look at the list."

Jane sighed, clearly relieved that Carlos had said that. She looked pretty impatient herself.

Carlos felt excitement rising inside him. This was it! The big list! He was about to see what he'd be spending the rest of that beautiful Saturday searching for.

With a deep breath, Carlos scrolled down and read the list.

THE ANNUAL
AURADON PREP
SCAVENGER HUNT LIST

1. A puppet made of wood—5 points
2. A slipper made of glass—5 points
3. A picture of your team posing in the display window of Belle's Boutique—10 points
4. An Auradon Express train ticket originating in Charmington—20 points
5. A violet-gold pixie fork—25 points
6. A selfie with Grumpy—25 points
7. The recipe for the "gray stuff" from Lumiere's Bistro—20 points
8. Fruit picked from a hazelberry tree—25 points
9. A perfect yellow rose—15 points
10. An Auradon Prep gym T-shirt from at least 20 years ago—15 points
11. A bowl of Tiana's famous gumbo—25 points

FETCH

I'm not so sure about this list.
Some of the items are easy. But
some don't even make sense!

Carlos stared at the list in awe. What was a violet-gold pixie fork? And where on earth were they supposed to find an Auradon Prep gym T-shirt from at least twenty years earlier? But no matter—they would figure it out. Carlos decided the best strategy was to start at the top of the list and work their way down. He already knew where they could find a puppet made of wood and a slipper made of glass.

Except they couldn't leave until their entire group was there, and there was still no sign of—

"Oh my gosh! I'm sorry! I'm so sorry!" Evie burst into the banquet hall pink-cheeked and breathless, like she'd just run laps around the tourney field. "I'm here." She glanced around the empty room in confusion. "Where is everyone?"

"They've all already left on the hunt," Carlos said, trying to keep the sharpness out of his tone. She really *did* look sorry. But that didn't change the fact that they were the only team left in the banquet hall, which meant they were already behind.

"Oh!" Evie said. "Sorry. You guys could have started without me. I could have caught up."

"Actually, we couldn't have," Carlos said. "The rule is that we have to stick together the entire time."

"Oh," Evie said again, cringing. "Well, I'm here now. Let's go! Let's win that trophy!"

Carlos sighed. "It's not a trophy. It's an engraved stone in the courtyard."

Evie bit her lip. "Oh, right. I forgot."

Carlos was frustrated with Evie, but he told himself to let it go. She was there now and that was all that mattered. So what if they were a little behind? They could catch up. And he was sure whatever reason Evie had for being late was a good one. She wasn't the kind of person to let her friends down.

"Okay," Carlos said, clapping his hands together and assuming his best team captain voice. "Let's do this. We have eleven things to collect on this list and only five hours to do it. And some of them are very hard."

Jane piped up. "Actually, I think maybe we should strategize and figure out which items to focus on. No one has ever gotten *all* the things on the list."

Carlos flashed Jane a smug grin. "That's only because *I've* never competed before. I fully intend to get every single thing on this list." Carlos was confident he could achieve it. And hearing Jane say that it had never been done before only made him want it more. He didn't want just to win the competition; he wanted to win by a landslide. He didn't want just to beat the other teams; he wanted to *pulverize* them. If this was his one shot at proving himself a leader, he had to impress people. No, he had to *wow* them. And Carlos knew that collecting every single item on the list was the way to do it.

"I say we go big or go home!" Carlos said, pumping his fist in the air. "I say we go for *all* of them."

Jane looked like she was about to argue with Carlos, but then she shook her head, smiled, and said, "Okay! You're the captain!"

"That's right!" Carlos said, beaming at the title. "I'm the captain. Now let's go get 'em, team! Are we ready?"

Carlos expected a rallying shout from his teammates, but the only one who responded was Jane. Carlos glanced around for Evie and saw that she had ducked into a corner and was tapping into her phone, her brow furrowed.

Carlos groaned. "Evie! I'm trying to lead us in a battle cry."

"Sorry!" Evie said without looking up from her tapping. "Just two . . ." *Tap. Tap. Tap.* "More . . ." *Tap. Tap. Tap.* "Seconds . . ." *Tap. Tap. Tap.*

She pressed a final key with a flourish. "And done!" Evie slipped her phone into her pocket. "All finished. I'm ready to go! Battle cry? Let's do it! *Hiyaaa!*"

Carlos slouched. "Never mind. The moment has passed. Let's just go."

HOT ON THE TRAIL

First stop: Geppetto's workshop.
It's almost too obvious that we'd
go there to find a puppet made
of wood. No wonder this one
is only worth five points.

Not only did they have plenty of marionettes to choose from, but the young man working at Geppetto's was nice enough to take a photo of the entire team holding one of the puppets. Carlos saved the photo to his phone, and the team rushed out.

Next they headed to the Museum of Cultural

History, where they were easily able to snap a photo of Cinderella's glass slipper, which was on display in one of the exhibits.

So far, so good, Carlos thought as they ran out of the museum. They already had ten points!

"Where to next?" Jane asked.

"Ooh!" Evie said. "I think I know where we might find a hazelberry tree. It's right near—"

"We're moving on to number three," Carlos announced, interrupting Evie. "Let's head to downtown Auradon to take the picture in the display window of Belle's Boutique."

Evie perked up. "Belle's Boutique? Oh, great! I really need to pick up some lace there and maybe a few extra buttons for—"

"We're not shopping, Evie," Carlos snapped, and then reminded himself to chill. He flashed a smile. "I mean, we don't have time. We need to stay focused."

"Right, focused," Evie said, but right as she said it, her phone beeped and she immediately glanced down at the screen, let out a frustrated sigh, and started typing.

Carlos did his best to stay calm. What was so important that Evie couldn't spend a few hours on a scavenger hunt? It was actually kind of strange. Evie wasn't normally that distracted.

Is something wrong? Carlos wondered. *Should I ask her about it?*

But he decided they didn't have time. He would have to ask Evie later.

As soon as they arrived at Belle's Boutique, Carlos knew that task wasn't going to be simple. They had to get a picture of all of them posing inside the display window, but the shopkeeper—a cranky elderly woman—saw them walk into the store and immediately pointed toward the door. "Oh, no. No more Auradon Prep students taking photos in my window. I've had ten teams in here already."

Carlos felt panic flare in his chest. "Please, ma'am. We really need this photo."

But she shook her head. "No way. The last team completely messed up my window display."

Evie tilted her head toward the display window, her lips pursed thoughtfully. "Hmmm. I could help you fix the display. You really should be highlighting more of this season's dresses, anyway. Bright yellows are totally in. And maybe some—"

"Evie," Carlos whispered, growing impatient. "We don't have time to be dressing windows. We have to get all of the items on the list by three o'clock."

"Yes, but—" Evie tried to argue, but Carlos cut her off.

"C'mon, let's go." He led Evie and Jane out of the store, and they stood on the sidewalk, staring at the window. "We need a plan."

"Maybe we should move on to the next item on the list," Jane suggested.

"No." Carlos immediately shot her down. "We're not skipping any. We just need to figure out a way to convince the shopkeeper to let us take the photo. Evie, do you have any ideas?"

But Evie wasn't listening. She was back to typing something on her phone, completely distracted again.

Distracted.

Carlos was suddenly struck with an idea. "I've got it! I'll call the store, pretending to be the water department. I'll tell her there's a leak in the alley behind her store. Then, when she goes out the back door, we'll go in the front. We'll snap the photo and get out of there before she returns."

"Great!" Jane commended him. "Well done. No wonder my mom chose you as captain!"

Carlos felt a small jab of guilt at the compliment, because he knew Fairy Godmother hadn't really chosen him. Carlos had commanded her to choose him while he was wearing the magic dog collar. But he told himself it didn't matter. What mattered now was how he handled himself. And he had to admit that so far he was doing a pretty awesome job. They'd already knocked two things off the list.

"Okay," Carlos said, "first we'll need to set up

my phone across the street to take the picture. We can set the timer to give us enough time to get inside the store and pose in the window. I'll make the call to the shop owner on Evie's phone. Evie?"

Evie glanced up from her phone screen, looking startled at hearing her own name. "Huh?"

"Can I borrow your phone?"

"Um . . ." she said hesitantly. "I'd really rather you not. I'm waiting for an important e-mail."

"Here," Jane said, offering her phone to him. "You can use mine."

"Thanks." Carlos propped his own phone on a small brick wall across the street from Belle's Boutique, angling it so it had the perfect view of the display window. Then, using Jane's phone, he dialed the number for Belle's Boutique. When the shopkeeper answered, Carlos lowered his voice a full octave, impersonating an adult. "Hello there. This is . . . um . . . Gustav McManister from the City of Auradon Water Department. I'm sorry to inform you that we've had reports of a leak in the alley behind your store."

Jane stifled a giggle, which almost made Carlos burst out laughing. He had to turn away from her to keep a straight face.

"A leak?" the shopkeeper said, sounding skeptical. "I was just out there a few minutes ago. There was no leak."

Carlos hesitated, trying to think fast. "Um, yes, well, the leak seems to be . . ." He glanced at Belle's Boutique, scanning the building for some kind of inspiration. That was when Jane tugged on his sleeve and pointed to a set of stairs leading to an underground level of the shop.

"Originating from the basement," Carlos said into the phone.

Apparently, those were the magic words, because the shopkeeper let out a panicked shriek. "The basement? But all of our inventory is stored in the basement."

"Yes, well, you'd better get down there right away," Carlos said, giving Jane and Evie a thumbs-up.

Jane crept across the street and peered in

through the shop window. When the shopkeeper had disappeared down the stairs, Jane signaled to Carlos. Carlos set the timer on the phone for thirty seconds and programmed it to take five photos. He figured that should be enough to capture them in the window.

He motioned to Evie that they should go, then darted across the street and joined Jane at the front door. He was about to walk into the store when he noticed that Evie was still standing next to the brick wall, tapping into her phone again.

"Evie!" Carlos called, covering the mouthpiece of Jane's phone so the shopkeeper wouldn't hear. "We have less than half a minute!"

"Coming!" she said. Without looking up from her screen, she hurried across the street and followed Carlos and Evie into the shop.

"There's no leak down here!" Carlos heard the shopkeeper say into the phone as the three of them headed for the window.

"Um, yes there is!" Carlos said desperately.

"You need to look harder. For at least another ten seconds!"

Carlos and Jane assumed poses in the window, pretending to be mannequins.

"Uh-oh," Jane said, wrinkling her nose. "There's too much perfume in this shop. It's making my nose tickle. I think I'm going to sneeze! This happened when I was interning for Carina Potts. We gave out French perfume for party favors at Esmeralda's birthday bash, and I was sneezing all night."

"Don't sneeze," Carlos ordered her. "At least not until we get the picture."

"Ah, ah, ah," Jane said, waving her hand in front of her nose. Carlos held his mannequin position, praying that Jane could hold her sneeze. A second later, he realized that Evie was not with them. She was still standing to the side of the display window, typing on her phone. "Evie! The timer is about to go off!"

"Be right there!" Evie said brightly.

Carlos marched over to Evie and began to pull her toward the window.

"Achooo!" Jane sneezed so loud even the shopkeeper heard it.

"What was that?" the shopkeeper barked over Jane's phone. "I don't have time to spend down here looking for an imaginary leak. I have customers upstairs."

Carlos heard footsteps on the stairs. He quickly dragged Evie into the window and told everyone, "Pose like a mannequin! Quick!" Evie glanced up long enough to flash a smile before she returned to her phone.

"I think we got it," Carlos said. The footsteps on the stairs got louder. "C'mon. Let's go."

"Two more seconds," Evie said, typing furiously.

Carlos urged her. "Evie, we don't have two more—"

"Hey!" came a cranky voice. "What are you kids doing in here? I thought I told you to stay out of my window!"

"Run!" Carlos commanded. Fortunately, both members of his team listened to him this time, and all three of them darted from the boutique with the shopkeeper close on their tails. When they reached the outside, she closed the door behind them with a bang. "I don't want to see you three scoundrels in my shop again!"

Carlos breathed a sigh of relief. "Whoa. That was close. Good thing we got the photo." But then his face fell into a frown when he picked up his phone and clicked on the five photos the camera had taken. There wasn't a single one that had captured all three of them. Three photos showed Carlos dragging a reluctant Evie into the window, and in the other two, all that was visible was the top of Jane's head as she sneezed.

ROLL OVER

More like keep on rollin'. This is just a
small hiccup. Nothing to worry about.

Carlos decided it was probably best to go back to
Belle's Boutique later in the day, after the shopkeeper had had a chance to cool down. Perhaps
after *Carlos* had had a chance to cool down, too.
Carlos was pretty frustrated with Evie. It was all
her fault they hadn't gotten the photo. If she hadn't
been on her phone, and had posed in the shop
window with Carlos and Jane, they would have
ten more points right now.

But Carlos told himself to let it go and focus

on the next item on the list. Evie had been really apologetic about the whole thing, and he could tell she meant it. Although he was still curious about what she kept doing on that phone.

Now they were on their way to the Auradon Express train station to try to score a picture of a ticket originating in Charmington.

Carlos checked the clock on his phone. It was almost noon. They'd wasted nearly two hours collecting ten measly points. But the Charmington train ticket was a big one. It was worth twenty points. Carlos felt confident it would help them catch up.

Jane had already checked the Auradon Express website (thanks to Carlos's clever thinking) and discovered that a train from Charmington was due into the station in ten minutes. All they had to do now was wait for the passengers to disembark the train and ask one of them if they could take a picture of their ticket.

Carlos saw no reason why that would be a problem.

That is, until they reached the train station.

Apparently, Carlos wasn't the only one with the clever idea to check when the next train from Charmington was going to arrive, because the train platform was overflowing with kids from Auradon Prep. They were gathered around the track, waiting for the train with their camera phones ready.

"Now what?" Jane asked, her eyes widening at the sight of all the students.

Carlos pushed his shoulders back. He wasn't going to lose hope. "We'll just have to be assertive and make sure we're able to get a picture of someone's ticket."

Carlos glanced around at the crowded train platform. He spotted Jay, Mal, and Lonnie huddled around Jay's phone, most likely counting up their current score. Carlos was desperate to find out how many points they had. He had no idea where his team stood right then with their ten points. Were they somewhere near the top of the pack? Or near the bottom?

"Wait right here," Carlos told Jane and Evie. "I'll be right back. I just want to . . . um, check something."

"But we're not supposed to split up," Jane pointed out. "And the train is arriving any minute."

"It's okay," Carlos assured her. "I'll be close by." Then Carlos darted off to the other side of the platform, where Jay's team was standing. Along the way, he grabbed an *Auradon Times* newspaper from the stand next to the display case and opened it up wide, so he could hide his face behind it. He didn't want Jay or Mal or Lonnie to see him snooping. But he had to know. A good team captain always kept track of the competition. Like how Jay always knew who the best tourney players were on all the other teams and what their signature moves were.

Keeping the newspaper in front of his face, Carlos inched closer to the group. They were still huddled close together, looking at something on Jay's phone.

Jay was speaking in a hushed tone. "Okay, so with the Belle's Boutique picture, the slipper made of glass, the puppet made of wood, and the yellow rose, that brings our score to thirty-five points."

Carlos cringed. Jay's team had thirty-five points already? And Carlos's team only had ten? If Jay's team was any indication of how the rest of the school was doing, Carlos really needed to step up his game. Even if his team was able to score the Auradon Express train ticket, no doubt Jay's team would, too, and they'd still be twenty-five points behind.

"We really need to figure out how to get Grumpy to pose for a selfie," Lonnie said. "That's a massive twenty-five points."

"Not gonna happen," Mal said. "Doug was telling me that his uncle Grumpy *hates* getting his photo taken. Like with a passion. There's a reason Fairy Godmother gave that the max amount of points. It's because it's impossible. No one is ever going to be able to convince him to do it, so we may as well just forget that one."

"What about the recipe for the gray stuff?" Jay asked. "How hard will that be?"

"It depends on what kind of mood Lumiere is in today," Lonnie said. "He doesn't like giving out his secret recipes."

Jay turned to Mal. "You're dating Belle and Beast's son. Do you think he'll give you special treatment?"

Mal shrugged. "It's worth a shot."

Carlos felt dread coating his stomach. Jay's team seemed so much more on top of things than his team. They were all involved, making an effort, suggesting ideas. Meanwhile, he couldn't even get Evie to glance away from her phone long enough to take a picture!

Just then, Carlos heard the whistle of a train and Jay's team broke out of their huddle and faced the track. Carlos inched back to his teammates just as the lights of the train started to appear around the bend in the track.

"Okay, team," Carlos said to Jane and Evie. "We really need this. Let's not mess it up." He looked pointedly at Evie when he said this, but of course she didn't even notice, because her face was buried in her phone again.

Carlos shook his head and sighed as he stood next to Jane, watching as the train approached the station with an earsplitting screech of tires on metal.

"As soon as you see a passenger get off the train, run up to them and ask to take a picture of their ticket."

Jane nodded. "Got it."

But before the train could even reach the station, Carlos was distracted by a strange sound coming from the next platform. It was soft at first, but getting louder by the second. Carlos couldn't be certain, but he thought it sounded a lot like a child crying.

MYSTERY WHIMPER

What is that sound?

Carlos glanced anxiously between the incoming train and the next platform. He tried to peer over the heads of all the other Auradon Prep students waiting to bombard the passengers getting off the train, but he couldn't see what was making that sound.

"Hold on," Carlos said, and took a few steps toward the adjoining platform.

"Carlos," Jane said. "The train is almost here!"

But Carlos didn't stop. He could hear the sound better now. It definitely sounded like someone crying. It was being washed out by the hissing of the incoming train.

Carlos took three more steps through the crowd, and that's when he saw the boy. He was huddled on the ground in the middle of the empty platform, sobbing. He looked to only be about six or seven years old. The boy's hair was white, just like Carlos's, which surprised Carlos. He had never before seen another child with white hair.

Carlos blinked, and for a second, he couldn't see the boy anymore. He only saw himself. A scared little boy, huddled inside his mom's fur-storage closet, crying to be let out. He felt a wave of fear pass through him, as though he were back there in that closet.

"Carlos!" Jane said, bringing him back to the train station. "What's going on?"

"We have to help him," Carlos said dazedly.

"Help who?" Jane asked, confused. But then she glanced in the direction where Carlos was staring and saw the boy. "Oh my gosh! What's wrong with him?"

Carlos shook his head. "I don't know. But we can't just stand here." And then he was moving, calling back to Jane and Evie to come with him. Carlos could hear the hiss of the train from Charmington as it pulled into the station, but he didn't care. This was more important.

When he reached the crying boy, he skidded to a halt and knelt down next to him. "Hey, hey, little guy," he said in a soothing voice. A voice he'd never heard from his mother. "What's the matter?"

The boy looked up. His face was tearstained. His eyes were red and puffy. He blinked, looking confused, as though he couldn't quite believe what he was seeing. "Carlos?" the boy asked.

Now Carlos looked confused. "Do I know you?"

In answer to the question, the boy leapt up and threw his arms around Carlos's neck in a hug. Carlos didn't know what to do. He certainly didn't recognize the boy. He patted him awkwardly on the back and glanced up at Jane, who had arrived with Evie.

Jane threw her hands up, as if to ask, *What did I miss?*

But Carlos only shook his head.

The boy sniffled into Carlos's leather jacket. "Carlos! I can't believe it's really you. Mommy said we wouldn't see you if we came to Auradon. That it was too big of a city and the chances of running into you were so small. But I knew we would see you. I just knew it!"

Carlos, still baffled by the exchange, pulled back so he could look into the boy's eyes. He searched the kid's face for a sliver of familiarity, but once again, he found nothing. "How do I know you?" Carlos asked.

The boy shook his head, his eyes still full of tears. "You don't."

"Okaaaay," Carlos said. This was getting stranger and stranger. "Then how do *you* know *me*?"

"Are you kidding?" the boy exclaimed. "You're my hero!"

Carlos snorted. "I think you have me confused with someone else."

But the boy shook his head adamantly. "No. It's you. *You're* my hero. I heard about you when you first came to Auradon from the Isle of the Lost. You were on TV and in the newspaper. You're so cool. You're my favorite VK." Then the boy seemed to notice Evie standing there for the first time and his eyes went wide. "Sorry!" he said to Evie, looking caught out.

Evie smiled a tender, caring smile. "No apology necessary. I agree. Carlos is pretty cool."

"What's it like at Auradon Prep?" the boy asked Evie. "Is it amazing? My daddy went to Auradon Prep a long time ago. I can't wait until I can go!"

Evie smiled. "It *is* pretty amazing."

"What are you doing in this train station all alone?" Carlos asked.

This seemed to remind the boy why he was crying in the first place. His eyes filled with tears again, and he tipped his head back and started wailing. He sounded like he was trying to say something but his words were choked by sobs.

"Shhh," Carlos said, trying to calm him down. "Shhh. It's going to be okay. Slow down. Take a deep breath."

The boy did as Carlos said, finally managing to form coherent words. "I lost my mommy."

"Awww." Jane knelt down next to the boy. "It's okay. Don't worry. We'll help you find her. Right, guys?" Jane looked at Carlos and Evie.

"Of course!" Evie said.

Carlos glanced at the next platform and could see that the train from Charmington had come to a stop and the doors were opening. He knew if they helped this boy, they might lose their chance at an Auradon Express train ticket. They might lose their chance at twenty points. A very *crucial* twenty points.

"Carlos?" Jane said.

Carlos shook his head. He was being ridiculous. He couldn't just leave this little boy to fend for himself. That would make Carlos no better than his mother. They'd just have to make up the points another way. Maybe there'd be another train from Charmington arriving later in the day.

"Of course we'll help you." Carlos stood and extended his hand for the little boy to take. The boy looked in disbelief between Carlos's hand and Carlos's face, a grin the size of Triton's Bay appearing on his lips. He took Carlos's hand, and Carlos helped him to his feet. The boy was wearing black-and-white leather pants that looked a lot like Carlos's. On top, he had on a ratty old blue T-shirt that was about four sizes too big, with the words RAD REP printed across the front in faded yellow letters. Carlos assumed "rad rep" must be some kind of popular Auradon kid thing he'd never heard of.

As Carlos led the boy into the train station, he glanced back at Jane, who was beaming with pride. He flashed her a wink and she winked back.

"First, I have to ask you the most important question of all," Carlos said to the boy.

The boy gaped up at him with joyous anticipation, as though waiting for an edict from King Ben himself. "What?"

Carlos squeezed his hand. "What's your name?"

LOST PUP

The kid's name is Henry, and
fortunately, it didn't take long
for us to find his mother.

Carlos and his team learned Henry and his mom
had been separated when getting off a train from
Grimmsville, where they lived. His mother had
been worried sick, searching all over the train station. When she saw her little boy being led over by
Carlos, Evie, and Jane, she let out a yelp of relief
and ran to them, scooping up the boy in her arms
and kissing his face over and over.

Carlos felt happy watching Henry be reunited with his mother, but he also felt a twinge of jealousy. His own mother never ran to him like that. Never scooped him up in her arms like that. His mother never showed him any affection. She barely paid him any attention unless she needed him to run an errand for her or scrape the bunions from her feet.

"Thank you!" Henry's mother said to the team after setting her little boy down. She turned to Carlos and did a double take. "Wait a minute, are you . . ."

"Yes, Mommy!" the boy chirped. "It's him! It's Carlos De Vil!"

The mother's smile tripled in size. "Well, what do you know? It is him! What a wonderful day this is." She turned to Carlos. "He's your biggest fan. He's really into computers. When he found out you were, too, you became his hero."

"Can we take a picture? Can we? Can we? Can we?" The boy started jumping up and down, tugging on his mother's hand. "Please! Please! Please!"

Carlos couldn't help chuckling. "Okay by me, bro."

The mother pulled her phone out of her purse and went to turn on the screen. Her face fell with disappointment. "Oh, no. Sweetie, I'm so sorry. My battery is dead."

The boy looked like someone had just told him fairies weren't real.

"That's okay," Carlos said, stepping in to save the day once again. He pulled his own phone out and handed it to Jane. "We can use mine and I'll send the picture to you. How's that?"

The boy's mother flashed Carlos another grateful smile, and Carlos and Henry posed in the center of the beautiful glass-walled train station. Carlos got down on one knee so he was the same height as Henry. He put his arm around Henry's shoulders and beamed toward the camera. Jane snapped the photo.

After sending the photo to Henry's mom and saying their good-byes, Carlos and his team returned to the platform where they'd been waiting for the Charmington train.

Carlos's shoulders sagged when he saw that the platform was completely deserted. The train had emptied and all the passengers had left. The students who had been milling around, waiting to take photos of tickets, were also gone.

They were all twenty points richer now.

And Carlos's team was, once again, leaving empty-handed.

LICKING THE WOUNDS

I'm super bummed. We just lost
a bunch of points we needed.
This is not going as planned.

Ten minutes later, Jane, Carlos, and Evie were sitting in an outdoor café in downtown Auradon, having lunch. Carlos was eating a sandwich, Jane was sipping on a smoothie, and Evie was, of course, typing something into her phone. Carlos hadn't even wanted to stop for lunch. They'd already wasted enough time that day, but Jane had been insistent.

"You need to eat," she'd said. "You need your strength. A captain is no good on an empty stomach."

At that very moment, Carlos's stomach had growled and he'd given in. Jane sort of had a point. Plus, they needed to regroup and come up with their next plan. They still had only ten points and he was certain Jay's team had at least fifty-five, if not more by now.

"I can't believe how far behind we are," Carlos muttered as he took a sip of his chocolate milk.

"Yeah, but it was worth it," Jane said. "Just look how cute you two are." She had been scrolling through photos on Carlos's phone and now turned it around so he could see the picture of him and Henry on the screen. "Look at his smile. You're like a celebrity to him!"

Carlos scoffed. Some celebrity he was. He couldn't even manage to get more than ten points in a scavenger hunt. He stared at the photo, focusing on the boy's T-shirt and leather pants. With the matching white hair and those pants, Carlos and Henry could easily pass as brothers. Henry had called Carlos his hero, but Carlos certainly didn't feel like a hero right then. He felt like a failure.

"This reminds me of a time when I was interning for Carina Potts and we threw a big birthday bash for John Darling's son. He was turning seven. All the kids there were so adorable."

"Carina Potts is my idol," Evie said, finally setting her phone down. "She's such a savvy businesswoman. You are so lucky to have landed an internship with her. What was it like? Was it the best summer of your life?"

Jane's face fell. "Actually, no. Not really."

Evie looked confused. "What? Why not? She's supposed to be *brilliant*."

"She is," Jane said. "I just don't think she thought *I* was very brilliant."

Carlos's gaze whipped toward Jane. "What? That's impossible. Didn't you spend like an entire weekend organizing her party supply inventory? And didn't you stay up until three in the morning weaving flowers into a garden wall?"

Jane shrugged. "Yeah, but she must not have thought I did a very good job. She never gave me a single compliment all summer."

"Jane," Evie began gently, but it was clear Jane didn't want to talk about it anymore, because she quickly interrupted Evie.

"That's all in the past. It doesn't matter. Let's focus on the scavenger hunt." Then she flashed Evie and Carlos a smile that Carlos could instantly tell was fake.

"Okay," Carlos said warily, wondering if he should let this go. But it was clear from Jane's expression that she was finished talking about it. He made a mental note to bring it up later, after the hunt was over. "Let's review the list again and decide what to go after next." He took his phone back from Jane and clicked on the message from Fairy Godmother he'd received that morning.

He scanned the first two items on the list:

1. A puppet made of wood—5 points
2. A slipper made of glass—5 points

They already had both of those. Carlos continued farther down.

3. A picture of your team posing in the display window of Belle's Boutique—10 points

He quickly skipped over that one, not wanting to be reminded of Evie's failure to listen to him in the shop. He was still pretty frustrated about that.

4. An Auradon Express train ticket originating in Charmington—20 points

That one was now a lost cause. After Henry and his mother had left the train station, Carlos had checked the information screens hanging in the terminal. The next train from Charmington wouldn't arrive until seven o'clock at night. By then it would be too late. Which meant all hopes of getting number four on the list were gone. Carlos sighed and moved on.

5. A violet-gold pixie fork—25 points

Carlos looked hopefully up at his team. "Does anyone know what a violet-gold pixie fork is? It's worth twenty-five points."

Evie shook her head. "No clue."

He then looked to Jane who, for some reason, wouldn't meet Carlos's eye. She was staring intently at the straw in her smoothie. Maybe she was still thinking about Carina Potts. "I think we should skip that one," she said quietly. "It sounds hard."

Carlos frowned and turned back to the list.

6. A selfie with Grumpy—25 points

Carlos thought back to the conversation he'd overheard on the train platform, among the members of Jay's team. Mal had said that convincing Grumpy to take a selfie would be impossible. But Carlos had to wonder if that was true. Twenty-five points would help his team a *lot*. It would put them at thirty-five, only twenty points behind Jay's team, assuming they hadn't already scored any other big items.

He glanced up at Evie, who had buried her face back in her phone. Her brows were furrowed and the salad in front of her was completely untouched.

"Evie," Carlos said.

"Hmm?" Evie replied without looking up.

"Do you think you can talk Grumpy into taking a selfie with us? You *are* dating his nephew."

Evie immediately shook her head. "No way. No how. That man is *adamantly* against photos of any kind. The only thing he hates more than photos is laughter. We should forget about that one because *no one* in the competition is going to get those points. It would take an act of magic to convince him to take that selfie."

Carlos scowled and continued to the next item on the list:

7. The recipe for the "gray stuff" from Lumiere's Bistro—20 points

But he couldn't quite concentrate on any of the words on his screen, because something Evie had said was ringing in his ears.

It would take an act of magic to convince him to take that selfie.

An act of magic . . .

Carlos quickly glanced at the screen on his phone and reread number six on the list—the recipe for the gray stuff from Lumiere's Bistro. He remembered Lonnie saying that, too, was near impossible. Lumiere rarely ever gave out recipes.

Suddenly, Carlos felt an idea forming in the back of his mind. An idea that would involve doing something he'd sworn to himself he would not do. But they were desperate. They were running out of time. They only had three more hours until the scavenger hunt was over, and they were way behind the other teams.

They just needed a little boost. A little shortcut. A *teensy* bit of help. To get them back on track.

"You know," Evie said, setting down her phone, "like I was saying before, I think there's a hazelberry tree on campus. We could go check it out and see about getting number eight."

But Carlos dismissed her idea with a wave of his hand. "Actually, I have a plan!"

"Great!" Jane said, slurping up the last of her smoothie. "Let's go!" Carlos stared at her. Was it just his imagination, or did Jane seem a little *too* eager to leave the café?

Carlos pushed his chair back from the table. "We just need to make a quick stop at my dorm room first."

DOG WITH A BONE

I can't let go of the idea to
use the collar to help. We just
need to make up some points and
catch up to the other teams.

"I don't understand what we're doing here," Evie complained as they stood on the doorstep of Grumpy's small one-story wooden cottage. "I already told you, he's not going to agree to this. This is a waste of time."

Carlos inconspicuously touched the red dog collar he'd slipped onto his wrist and hidden under the sleeve of his jacket. "I'm feeling lucky." He knocked hard on the door.

Evie raised an eyebrow. "Luck has nothing to do with it. According to Doug, the guy is very disagreeable."

Just then, the door swung open and Carlos, Evie, and Jane all looked down at the small man standing in front of them with his arms crossed. "What do you think you're doing banging on my door at one o'clock in the afternoon?" he barked.

"I'm sorry, sir," Jane was quick to say. She was always the first to try to smooth out a rough situation. "We were hoping that we might be able to take a selfie with you."

Grumpy huffed. "A what?"

"A selfie," Jane repeated, pronouncing the word slowly.

"What on earth is that?" Grumpy blustered.

"Oh!" Evie perked up, clearly wanting to be the one to explain this particular cultural phenomenon. "It's this great invention where you hold the camera up like this"—she positioned her phone in front of her face and gave her hair a toss—"and you take a photograph of your*self*. See? *Self*ie." She flashed a warm smile at the dwarf until her phone beeped with an incoming message and she lowered the device to read it. "Sorry, just gotta take this real quick."

"I don't take photos with kids," Grumpy grunted.

"Oh, that's okay," Jane said. She was smiling so big it looked like she was straining her face. "Because we're not technically kids. We're teens. So it's different."

"I don't take photos with teens," Grumpy said, his arms still crossed defiantly over his chest. Carlos noted that he really did look pretty unhappy.

"It's for a good cause," Jane tried.

Grumpy snorted. "If you want to serve a good cause, you'll get off my doorstep." He was about to close the door in their faces when Carlos stepped up and extended his arm to stop it.

"Carlos," Jane whispered warningly, "what are you doing? He said he won't do it."

Carlos flashed Jane a smile. "Let me give it a try." He bent down so he could look Grumpy in the eye. The dwarf stared back at him in challenge.

"Mr . . . um, Grumpy," Carlos began and then cleared his throat. "You see, we're competing in the annual Auradon Prep Scavenger Hunt and—"

"I don't care what you're competing in, I told you to get off my doorstep."

Evie, who had apparently just finished replying to her incoming message, tapped Carlos gently on the shoulder. "I think maybe we should go. This is exactly what I said would happen."

But Carlos ignored her. He gave his wrist a little shake, feeling the soft leather of the dog collar rub against his skin. "Like I was saying," he went on in an authoritative tone, "we're competing in the annual Auradon Prep Scavenger Hunt and we need to take a selfie with you. It's worth a lot of points, so I'm going to go ahead and *demand* that you man up—or *dwarf* up, or whatever—and take the picture with us."

Carlos's words were so bold and commanding, both Evie and Jane winced and looked at Grumpy, fully expecting him to explode with grumpiness. But he didn't. He stood there for a moment, his arms still crossed over his chest, and stared dazedly back at Carlos, as though he'd fallen asleep with his eyes open. Finally, he shrugged and said, "Okay, fine, but let's make it quick. My favorite TV show starts in a couple of minutes."

Evie's mouth fell open. Jane was rendered completely speechless. Carlos smiled and thanked the dwarf as he sidled up next to him and put his arm around Grumpy's shoulder. He clicked his phone camera to selfie mode and hoisted it high above his head. But when he looked at the screen, he saw that only he and Grumpy were in the shot. "Girls? Are you gonna get in here or what?"

The girls were both still standing there, staring at Carlos in absolute awe. They snapped to attention and ran over to Grumpy and Carlos, wedging themselves into the picture.

"Smile!" Carlos said. Evie and Jane both beamed up at the camera. Grumpy, who Carlos was certain was *not* used to smiling, made an effort to pull the corners of his mouth up. It looked more like a grimace then a smile, but it didn't matter. Carlos snapped the photo. And just like that, the twenty-five points were theirs.

"How did you do that?" Jane asked a few minutes later after they'd waved good-bye to Grumpy and thanked him profusely.

"Yeah," Evie echoed Jane's disbelief. "I never thought he'd *ever* agree to that."

Carlos shrugged, his confidence growing by the minute. "What can I say? I guess I'm just a natural-born leader."

TAIL WAGGING

The entire way to Lumiere's
Bistro, Evie and Jane couldn't stop
talking about my amazing feat.
I'm not going to lie; I'm loving the
praise and attention, even if I did
have a little help getting it.

When the group arrived at the restaurant and pushed open the door, they nearly crashed right into Jordan, Ben, and Chad, who were coming out, looking frustrated. "It's no use going in there," Jordan griped. "Lumiere is not giving out his secret recipe for the gray stuff."

Jane sighed and started to turn around. "Oh, well. Our little streak was fun while it lasted."

Carlos grabbed her gently by the arm and spun her back around. "We have to at least try."

"Didn't you hear me?" Jordan said. "He's not giving it out."

"It's true," Ben offered sympathetically. "We tried everything."

"*I* haven't tried yet," Carlos said smugly.

"Well, good luck," Chad said sarcastically. "Lumiere is best friends with Ben's parents, and if he wouldn't give the recipe to us, he's certainly not going to give it to two VKs."

Carlos shrugged, undeterred. "I don't know, I've been known to be pretty persuasive."

"It's true," Jane admitted. "You should have seen what he just did at—"

But Carlos quickly covered her mouth with his hand. "Shhh!"

Jane shot him a strange look. "What? What's wrong? Why can't I tell them?"

Carlos didn't want the whole school knowing

that he'd convinced Grumpy to take a selfie with them. It might raise suspicions. And he couldn't have a bunch of distrustful gazes pointed at him right now. The last thing he needed was to get caught using magic to win the scavenger hunt and get disqualified from the whole thing.

He smiled innocently at Jane. "We can't be giving away all our secrets."

Jordan rolled her eyes. "We don't care about your secrets. We're going to beat you guys anyway." Then she, Chad, and Ben hurried off into town.

Carlos reached for the door handle of the bistro.

"Don't you think we're wasting our time?" Evie asked, glancing up from yet another message on her phone. "If Ben couldn't get Lumiere to give up his recipe, what makes you think we can?"

"Now what kind of leader would I be if I let other people tell me what I can and can't do?" Carlos grinned and walked into the restaurant, just managing to catch the concerned glance Evie and Jane shared behind him.

The bistro was currently closed to diners. The waitstaff was busy setting the tables for dinner, positioning gorgeous china plates between sparkling silver knives and forks, shining up clear crystal goblets, and lighting long tapered candles in ornate brass candlesticks.

As soon as the group assembled inside, Lumiere came rushing out of the kitchen, babbling in his charming French accent. "Oh, no. No, no, no. Not anozer group of scavenger hunters. *S'il vous plait*, you must go. *Allez! Allez!*"

"If you'll just hear us out—" Carlos began to say, but Lumiere was quick to interrupt him.

"Like I told za last group, no one gets my secret recipe for za gray stuff. Not you, not Ben, not anyone."

Evie crossed her arms. "Why would Fairy Godmother put it on the scavenger hunt list if you're not going to give it out?"

Lumiere's expression soured. "Zat, I have no idea. But you're not getting eet. Eet's an old family recipe and I won't have eet floating around all of Auradon."

"We just need a picture of it," Jane said. "We promise to delete it as soon as the points are tallied."

Lumiere chuckled. "Zat's what za last group said, too. You Auradon students are quite za little negotiators, but my answer ees still no."

Carlos cleared his throat and pushed his way to the front of the group. "Let me handle this," he whispered over his shoulder to his teammates. He bowed to Lumiere. "Bonjour, monsieur," Carlos said with terrible pronunciation. "Lovely bistro you have here."

"Merci," Lumiere said tightly, his expression stern.

"We really need that recipe."

"And I told you—" Lumiere began, but Carlos held up a hand.

"Let me rephrase," Carlos said, twisting his

wrist until he felt the smooth, worn surface of the collar beneath his sleeve. "You *will* give us that recipe."

And right as Carlos said the words, Lumiere's gaze turned glassy. He stared at Carlos, his mouth slightly ajar, his head tilted. "I will give you zat recipe," he repeated. He snapped his fingers. "Jacques!" he called to one of the waiters. "Bring me za recipe for za gray stuff!"

"But monsieur . . ." Jacques argued, looking concerned.

"Maintenant!" Lumiere called out. "Now!"

Jacques scurried into the kitchen, returning a moment later with a heavy black leather book. He had it open to a page in the middle, which Carlos could see was a recipe. Jacques handed the book to Lumiere, and Lumiere proffered it to Carlos, his expression still vacant.

As Carlos pulled his phone out of his pocket and snapped the picture of the recipe, he could hardly contain his excitement. This was going to be another twenty points! They were really cruising now. But in his eagerness, Carlos's phone slipped from his fingers and, for a moment, seemed to be flying through the air in slow motion, tumbling around and around. Carlos dove for it. He couldn't risk the phone falling to the ground and breaking. They had too many of their photos for the hunt on it and he hadn't uploaded any of them to the Auradon Prep server yet.

Thankfully, Carlos managed to catch the phone before it hit the floor, but he was *not* able to catch himself before crashing into a waiter carrying a trayful of water glasses. The tray tumbled over and every single glass of ice water poured right onto Jane, completely drenching her. Jane screamed from the shock and cold.

"Oh, *mon dieu*," Lumiere said, rushing forward to help Jane.

"Don't worry," Carlos said, reaching her first. "I've got this." He put an arm around Jane's shoulders. She was soaking wet and shivering. He felt horrible. After all, he was the one who'd knocked into the waiter. Without a second thought, Carlos shrugged out of his leather jacket and draped it around Jane's shoulders.

"Thank you," Jane said through chattering teeth.

"C'mon," Carlos said, leading Jane toward the door. "Let's get you out in the sun where it's warmer."

But Jane didn't move. She seemed frozen to the spot. And before Carlos could ask what was wrong, he noticed something had caught Jane's attention. She was staring at Carlos's left arm.

"What is that?" Jane asked, and Carlos could hear a trace of accusation in her voice.

"What is what?" Carlos asked, confused.

"That." Jane stretched out her finger toward Carlos's wrist, and Carlos suddenly felt a chill rack his body, even though, unlike Jane, he was 100 percent dry.

Jane was pointing at the dog collar.

TAIL BETWEEN
MY LEGS

Uh-oh. I think I'm about to be in
trouble. And I probably deserve it.

"So, what do you say?" Carlos asked as they
stepped out of Lumiere's Bistro. "Should we try
to find a bowl of Tiana's world-famous gumbo?
Do they even serve that outside of the bayou? Or
maybe we should try to find that hazelberry tree
Evie was talking about. Does anyone know where
we can get an old Auradon Prep gym T-shirt?"
He was rambling now, and he knew it. But he just
couldn't bear to look at Jane. She was still staring
at his left wrist. He tried to cover the collar with

his right hand, but it was too late for that. Jane had seen it and she could clearly tell something was up.

"Carlos," Jane said, her voice curious, like she was trying to put the pieces together. "What is that?"

Evie glanced up from the message she was typing on her phone. She peered at the dog collar, which poked out from underneath Carlos's hand, and shrugged, seemingly not as concerned with the item as Jane was. "It looks like a dog collar. I like it. Very fitting for that whole *Dalmatian chic* look he's got going on. In fact, I really love it. I'm going to make a note to put more dog collar accessories in my next season's line." Then she went back to tapping on her phone.

Carlos looked hopefully to Jane, wondering if maybe Evie's little speech had convinced her to drop her suspicion, but Jane was too smart for that. And with magic in her blood, she could clearly sense something was going on here.

"Where did you get it?" Jane asked Carlos.

Carlos's immediate instinct was to lie. To tell

her he'd found it lying around somewhere. Or that he'd bought it in a store in downtown Auradon. This was his out, his chance to get off scot-free and continue with the hunt as though nothing had happened. But then Jane took a step toward him and captured his gaze with hers. Carlos looked into her big blue eyes and knew right away that he couldn't lie to her. Not to Jane. He cared too much about her. Besides, he wasn't on the Isle anymore. His days of lying and cheating were supposed to be over.

And yet here he was . . . a cheater. The proof was clasped right around his wrist. The guilt suddenly hit him like a punch in the chest.

Carlos closed his eyes. He couldn't look at her while he said it. He couldn't stand to see her reaction when he admitted to her that he'd cheated. That he'd fallen back into his old ways. That the temptation of winning—of proving something—had been too much for him. He just wanted to be seen as a leader.

And then, an unsettling thought struck Carlos.

Maybe I'm just not *a leader. Maybe my mom was right. Maybe I'll always be a sad, weak little follower. Maybe I just don't have what it takes to be a good team captain. After all, I had to cheat just to get us a few lousy points. Maybe I should just accept my fate as the forever sidekick. The nice guy who helps people out. That's all I'm really good for.*

Carlos sighed, and with his eyes still shut tight, he said, "I got it from my mother. It's a magic dog collar. She gave it to me before I left the Isle. Whoever wears it can convince anyone to do anything. Like a dog obeying its owner."

When Carlos finally found the courage to open his eyes, he looked first at Jane, then at Evie. Jane wasn't wearing the disappointed expression he was expecting to see. Her face was more pensive and thoughtful. Evie's was twisted in surprise.

"That's how you were able to convince Grumpy to take the selfie?" Evie asked.

Carlos nodded.

"And how you were able to convince Lumiere to give up the recipe," Jane concluded.

Carlos nodded again, feeling shame cover his whole body like a heavy fur coat.

"But . . . but . . ." Jane stammered, as though she were trying to find the right words. "But *why?* Is that really how you want to win this?"

Carlos sighed and looked at the ground. He kicked a stray pebble with the toe of his boot. "No . . . yes . . . I don't know! I just . . ." He stopped and tried to summon the strength to admit to his teammates what had been bothering him for the entire day, maybe even for his entire life. "I just wanted to be a great leader! I wanted to be more than just Carlos, the nice guy, everyone's best friend. The guy you come to when you need help with your computer. The guy you come to when you need advice about who to ask to the next ball. I'm never the guy you ask to be in charge." He felt his shoulders slouch. Getting all that off his chest was a relief, but the weight of what he had done was right there waiting to press down on him again.

Jane frowned and shared a look with Evie, as

though they were both trying to come up with the right words to say, but both were unable to find them.

"I'm not like you, Jane," Carlos went on. "Everyone thinks of *you* as a leader. Even with that app we have to design for Safety Rules for the Internet class. Everyone immediately turned to you when it was time to pick a project manager. No one ever turns to me for that kind of stuff."

Jane let out a sad little chuckle. "That's really sweet, Carlos, but no one turns to me because they think I'm a leader. They turn to me because I'm organized. And because of the internship I had with Carina Potts last summer. They assume I must know how to plan things." Jane grew quiet. "Although I don't think Carina Potts would agree with them."

"That's not true," Carlos said. "I'm sure you did an amazing job with that internship."

Jane shook her head. "You don't know that."

"I do," Carlos insisted. "Because I know you and I believe in you."

"And *we* believe in *you*," Jane was quick to reply.

She turned to Evie, who nodded. "Absolutely!"

Carlos scoffed. "Well, you shouldn't. Before I put on this collar, we'd scored a measly ten points! Ten! I've been failing at being a team captain all day. We missed the picture at Belle's Boutique. We missed the train ticket originating in Charmington—"

"Yes, but that was only because you helped Henry find his mother," Jane pointed out.

Carlos threw his hands up. "Exactly! We missed a huge item on the list because good ol' reliable Carlos had to go help someone. What a surprise."

"Are you saying you regret helping him?" Jane asked, baffled.

"No!" Carlos replied, feeling flustered. "Of course not. I just . . . this is the problem. I'm not a leader. And I may as well just accept that."

"That's not true," Evie said, stepping forward and putting a tender hand on Carlos's shoulder.

"The whole thing at Belle's Boutique was my fault. Not yours."

Carlos snorted. "Exactly. I can't even get *you*—one of my best friends—to listen to me. That's how horrible of a team captain I am. *You* won't even follow my lead." He nodded toward the pocket where Evie had stored her phone. "You clearly have better things to do than listen to what I have to say."

For a full ten seconds, Evie didn't respond. She just stared openmouthed and speechless at Carlos. Then, finally, after what felt like ages, she blurted out, "Oh my gosh, Carlos! No!"

Tears welled in her eyes, taking Carlos by surprise. He hadn't expected to make her cry. Now he felt even worse than he had before.

Evie walked over to a nearby bench and plopped down. She rubbed her hands under her eyes. "Carlos, this has nothing to do with you."

Sensing there was something bigger going on, Carlos sat down next to his friend. "Evie, what are you talking about? What's going on?"

Evie let out a shuddering breath. "It's . . . it's . . ." Then words started to flow out of her so fast Carlos had a hard time keeping up. It was as though she, too, was unburdening herself for the first time. Casting off everything that had been weighing her down. "It's my fashion company— Evie's Four Hearts. I messed up. Big-time. I was so busy and stressed out with all the orders for dresses that were coming in and all my school work, I made a huge mistake."

"What mistake?" Carlos asked. He hadn't heard anything about this.

Evie sniffled. "I accidentally placed an order for two hundred *slippers* instead of two hundred *zippers*. I needed the zippers for the dresses that people bought but instead I'm now stuck with a bunch of house slippers with bunnies on them. I've been emailing with the supplier all day trying to fix it. Not to mention all the customers I have to contact. Do you know how hard it is to tell a princess that her dress is delayed?"

Carlos chuckled politely. "I don't."

Evie sighed. "Well, they don't like it. And I've pretty much been doing that all day. I'm so sorry, Carlos. I feel horrible that you thought, even for a second, that this was about you. I think you have the ability to be a fantastic team captain. People *like* you and *respect* you." Evie grabbed his hand and squeezed it. "Trust me, I wouldn't want to be on *anyone* else's team but yours."

A moment later, Jane sat down quietly on the bench next to Carlos and grabbed his other hand. "Neither would I."

Carlos felt a swell of love for his friends pass through him, followed shortly by another wave of guilt. Even though he believed Evie and Jane, the fact remained: he'd still cheated. He'd still used magic to help his team earn points in the scavenger hunt. And now he didn't know what to do. He didn't know how to chase this guilty feeling away.

Carlos stood up and turned to Evie and then to Jane, flashing them both appreciative smiles. "Thank you guys. I couldn't have asked for better teammates."

"Where are you going?" Jane asked. Her voice was patient and kind. Jane was always so kind. It was what Carlos liked most about her.

"I don't know," Carlos admitted. "I just . . . I guess I need to think."

And before Jane or Evie could convince him to stay, Carlos took a deep breath, turned, and walked away.

It was true what he'd said. He didn't know where he was going. He just wandered aimlessly around downtown Auradon, thinking about everything that had happened that day.

As he walked, passing small shops and restaurants, Carlos rubbed his hand against the soft leather of the dog collar, feeling regret over what he'd done.

He knew he could never really win the competition now. It wouldn't feel right. He supposed he could just delete the photo of Grumpy and the photo of Lumiere's secret recipe, but that didn't feel like enough.

By the time he reached the entrance of the

Auradon Prep campus, Carlos knew what he had to do. He had a feeling his decision would disappoint his teammates, but it was his only option. Evie was right. Good leaders are trustworthy. And Carlos had broken that trust. Now he had to repair it.

And there was only one way to do that.

Carlos had to resign from the annual Auradon Prep Scavenger Hunt.

IN THE DOGHOUSE

I can't believe I'm doing this.
I know it's the right thing to
do . . . but then why does it feel
so bad? Why does it feel like I'm
letting my whole team down?

Carlos sat in Fairy Godmother's office, his knee
bouncing up and down like it had been spelled
with a fidgeting curse.

But it wasn't a curse, it was guilt. He'd let his
whole team down the moment he'd decided to put
on that dog collar. And he knew it.

"Carlos," Fairy Godmother said brightly.

"How are you? Are you enjoying your very first Auradon Prep Scavenger Hunt?"

Carlos swallowed hard. "I'm quitting the hunt."

Fairy Godmother flinched, as though someone had just poked her. "What? Why?"

Carlos spoke very fast, trying to get it all out before he lost his nerve. "Because I'm not a good team captain. I let my team down. They deserve someone better. I'm hoping you'll let them continue on without me, because it's not their fault. It's my fault. I'm the one who should be punished, not them. That's why I'm removing myself from the equation. Evie and Jane should be able to finish the hunt by themselves because—"

"Whoa, whoa," Fairy Godmother said, holding up a dainty hand. "Slow down, Carlos. Take a deep breath."

Carlos tried, but it felt like someone was standing on his chest.

"Okay, back up," Fairy Godmother instructed calmly. "Tell me what happened."

Carlos's gaze fell to the red dog collar strapped to his wrist. *My mother is what happened,* he thought glumly. *If she hadn't given me this dog collar, none of this would have happened.*

But even as Carlos thought it, he knew deep down that it wasn't true. This wasn't about his mother. This was about him. *He* was the one who had put the dog collar on. *He* was the one who hadn't trusted he could do it on his own. *He* was the one who'd cheated.

He slowly unclasped the collar and dropped it on Fairy Godmother's desk. The little bone-shaped tag made a tinkling sound as it clanked against the wood. Fairy Godmother's gaze slid toward the dog collar but she didn't say a thing. She was clearly waiting for Carlos to explain.

So he did. "My mother gave me this before I left the Isle. It has magical powers. When I wear it, I can give a command to anyone and they *have* to do what I say. They have no choice. I used it to command Grumpy to take a selfie with us. I used it to command Lumiere to give us the recipe for the gray stuff. And I used it to command you to make me team captain. I'm fake. I'm a phony. I don't deserve to be in this role. I'm not a true leader."

Then Carlos pulled his phone out of his pocket, swiped to the pictures of Lumiere's recipe and the selfie in front of Grumpy's house, selected them both, and pressed delete.

Fairy Godmother watched him with silent curiosity. She had still yet to utter a single word since he'd taken off the collar. Carlos nodded and started to stand up. "I guess I'll go now."

"Wait," Fairy Godmother said, raising a hand and then gently lowering it as a signal for Carlos to return to his seat. He did. "I commend your honesty," she said after a long pause. "And your willingness to forfeit your chance at a victory in order to do the honorable thing." She nodded toward his phone.

Carlos waited for her to continue. But the longer they sat there in silence, the more convinced he became that she was *not* going to continue.

That she had said her piece and that was that. He prepared to stand up again.

"However," Fairy Godmother announced, "I'm going to have to respectfully disagree with you."

Carlos furrowed his brow in confusion. "What?"

"When you said you are not a true leader. I disagree."

Carlos scoffed. Had she not listened to a single word he'd said? He'd cheated. He'd forced her to choose him as team captain. He'd used magic to get what he wanted. He was as far from a leader as you could get.

"When I chose you to be a team captain—" Fairy Godmother began, but Carlos quickly cut her off.

"That's the thing. I don't think you understand what I'm saying. I *made* you choose me. The collar made you choose me."

Fairy Godmother raised her hand in the air

once again to silence him. Carlos sighed but shut his mouth.

"That collar"—Fairy Godmother flicked her gaze toward the red leather item on her desk—"may have compelled Lumiere and Grumpy to do what you wanted, but it certainly didn't compel me."

Carlos stared at her, not following.

Fairy Godmother let out a blithe chuckle. "Carlos, I chose the team captains a week ago."

He blinked in disbelief. "What?"

She nodded. "So, like I was saying, when *I* chose you to be a team captain, I did it because I knew you had leadership potential. I've seen the way the other kids rely on you. They come to *you* for help more than they come to the teachers. They *adore* you, Carlos."

"Well, they certainly don't do what I say," Carlos muttered. He still couldn't bring himself to believe that Fairy Godmother had selected him all on her own.

Fairy Godmother chuckled again. "Is that what you think leadership is? Getting people to do whatever you say? Bossing people around? Convincing people to follow you blindly?"

Carlos frowned. "Sort of."

"That's what a *dictatorship* is," Fairy Godmother clarified.

"That's what my *mother* is," Carlos added with a dark laugh.

Fairy Godmother shot him a sympathetic look. "Leadership is about trusting your team. Protecting them. But most of all, leadership is about earning the respect of your team, which you already have. Almost the moment you arrived here, the students began to look up to you and *like* you. I recognized that a long time before you ever decided to use that collar."

Carlos glanced at the abandoned collar on Fairy Godmother's desk, his mind spinning. All this time he'd thought no one saw him as a leader. He thought they only saw him as a friendly helper.

But that wasn't true. There was at least *one* person who saw him as a leader: the headmistress of the whole school.

Fairy Godmother smiled, as though she could read Carlos's thoughts. "Being a captain of any team is not about bossing them around. It's about bringing them together, helping them find their strengths and then *using* those strengths. And that's exactly what I suggest you do." Fairy Godmother glanced at her watch. "But you better hurry, the hunt ends in less than two hours."

Carlos sighed and stood up, but then his brain registered what Fairy Godmother had said and his head whipped back toward her. "Wait, what?"

"I said you have less than two hours, so you'd better hurry."

"You mean . . ." he began, faltering. "You mean, I'm not disqualified from the competition."

Fairy Godmother reached out and pulled the dog collar toward her. "You surrendered this magical item. You came to me with the truth. You even deleted the pictures of the items you collected dishonestly. I would say, you've just proved to be the scavenger hunt's MVP."

MVP! Carlos repeated jubilantly in his mind. Fairy Godmother was calling *him* the most valuable player! Plus, she was giving him and his team another chance! He ran around the desk, wrapped his arms around her, and hugged her.

Fairy Godmother seemed startled by the sudden affection, but eventually she laughed and hugged him back.

"Jane's lucky to have a mother like you," Carlos said, emotion choking the words a little.

Fairy Godmother smiled. "And she's also lucky to have a friend like you." Then she shooed him away with her hand. "Now, go. Get back out there. Show us what you can do!"

Without wasting another second, Carlos bolted from the room.

BACK TO MY PACK

I'm gathering my team in the banquet hall, because it makes sense to go back to where we started—where this whole scavenger hunt veered off course. Back to the beginning for a do-over. Except now I'm going to handle things differently.

"Okay," he said, seating himself next to Jane at the table. "Let's come up with a strategy. I want everyone's input. We're going to conquer this thing together."

Evie smiled at Carlos like a proud older sister. Her empty hands were folded on the table in front of her. After Carlos had shared the good news with his team—that Fairy Godmother was allowing him to continue with the hunt—Evie had agreed to silence her phone and keep it in her pocket until the competition was over.

Carlos pulled up the scavenger hunt list on his phone and placed it in the center of the table so they could all see the screen. "Which items seem the most doable to you guys?"

Evie and Jane leaned in and peered at the list. "Let's forget number three," Evie said. "That shopkeeper at Belle's Boutique is going to shoo us away with a broom if we show our faces in there again."

"And we're never going to get a bowl of Tiana's gumbo with so little time," Jane said. "I had to special-order some during my internship."

"I wonder if we could find someone who had the recipe and make it ourselves," Evie suggested.

Jane shook her head. "Not enough time. The gumbo has to stew for at least two hours."

"Okay, no gumbo," Carlos said. "What about the fruit picked from the hazelberry tree? Evie, didn't you say you knew where a tree was?"

"Yes!" Evie said excitedly. "We studied the tree in botany class, and I think there's one near the dorms."

"What does the tree look like?" Carlos asked.

Evie pursed her lips, as if she was trying to picture it. "It's tall and thin, and the branches kind of stick out like . . . like . . ." She glanced up at Carlos. "Like your hair first thing in the morning."

Jane giggled.

"Har-har, very funny," Carlos said sarcastically.

"And the hazelberry fruit is sort of reddish-purplish, like a plum but bigger."

Carlos's eyes shot wide open. "Hold on a second. Did you say 'like a plum'?"

"Yeah, why?" Evie asked.

"There's a tree like that outside of Jay's and

my dorm room! I always wondered what it was. I thought it was a plum tree, but the fruit always looked so huge. I just thought maybe plums were bigger in Auradon."

Evie snapped her fingers. "That's right! I knew I'd seen one somewhere."

Carlos doubled-checked the list, feeling his hopes rise. The hazelberry fruit was a whopping twenty-five points. If they could nab that one, they'd be well on their way. Carlos wondered if Jay had remembered the tree, too. He hoped not.

"Well, what are we waiting for?" Carlos said, jumping to his feet. "Let's go berry picking!"

UNDERDOGS

We're back; we've got a new
plan; and I'm rooting for us!

Two minutes later, Carlos, Jane, and Evie burst
into Carlos's dorm room, completely out of breath.
Carlos couldn't remember ever having run up the
stairs that fast in his life. They all skidded to a halt
when they saw Jay and Mal standing by the open
window. Carlos's hopes fell. So Jay *had* remembered the hazelberry tree. That meant he was
probably only a few seconds away from scoring
another twenty-five points.

Jay and Mal both had their heads stuck out

the window, and they were shouting at someone. "A little to the left! Yes! You're almost there! You can do it!"

"I can't do it!" responded someone from outside. Carlos immediately recognized the voice as Lonnie's. "It's way too steep! I'm going to slip. I'm coming back in." A moment later, Mal and Jay stepped back from the window and Lonnie leapt inside, did an impressive somersault onto Jay's bed, and sprang to her feet like a gymnast.

She waved at Carlos, Evie, and Jane. "Hi, guys!"

At that moment Mal and Jay seemed to notice for the first time that they were standing there. Jay looked annoyed, presumably because Carlos's team had discovered the tree. "Don't bother," he mumbled. "The roof is too steep to get to the fruit, and the tree is too high to climb. We've already wasted enough time on it." Then he pushed past Carlos toward the door. "C'mon, team. Let's go. We're running out of time."

As Carlos watched Jay leave, a thought passed

through his mind. *He seems agitated.* Carlos wondered if perhaps Jay, too, was feeling the heat of the competition. Had he been unsuccessful in collecting as many items as he'd wanted? That gave Carlos an inkling of hope. The hazelberry fruit was one of the highest-valued items on the list. If Jay's team couldn't manage to get it but Carlos's team could . . .

"Eek," Jane squealed, interrupting Carlos's thoughts. He looked over to see Jane sticking her head out the window toward the hazelberry tree. "That looks impossible!"

Carlos and Evie both darted to the window and stuck their heads out next to Jane's. Carlos followed her gaze, and his stomach clenched with disappointment. She was right. It *did* look impossible.

The top of the tree was at least ten feet away from the window. There was no way anyone could reach out and pluck the fruit from a branch. That meant someone would have to climb out the window and scurry across the roof to get close enough to the tree. But the roof near the window was incredibly steep. No wonder Lonnie had dived back through. She had probably been scared out of her mind. And Lonnie was one of the most athletic students in Auradon. If she couldn't reach that tree, then there was really no hope for anyone else.

Carlos sighed as he ducked his head back into the room. "Well, there goes that idea." He reached into his pocket and pulled out his phone, then flipped back to the list. "What else is left to do?" He started to skim through the items again.

They'd already gotten numbers one and two. Number four—the Auradon Express train ticket—was out. There wasn't another train arriving from Charmington until later that night. Evie was right that number three—posing in the window of Belle's Boutique—was probably not their best option. He couldn't go back to Grumpy's house to try again at number six. "Maybe we should—" Carlos started, but he was cut off by Evie.

"Wait a minute," she said. Carlos turned and

saw that Evie still had her head stuck out the window. She seemed to be studying the roof with great intensity, tilting her outstretched hand at various angles as though she were trying to calculate the exact slope of the top of the building.

Then, without warning, she ducked her head inside and sprinted toward the door, calling over her shoulder, "I have an idea. But I need ten minutes."

Jane looked panicked. "We don't have ten minutes. The hunt is ending in *thirty* minutes!"

Carlos felt the same reaction rising in him. Jane was right. They were quickly running out of time. But he could hear Fairy Godmother's voice in his mind.

Leadership is about trusting your team.

"No," Carlos said, raising a hand. "Give her ten minutes."

Evie beamed. "Thanks, Carlos! I'll be right back!"

Jane and Carlos exchanged confused looks. "What is she doing?" Jane asked.

Carlos shrugged. "I have no clue. But whatever it is, I believe she can do it."

Evie returned less than a minute later, carrying a bag full of shoes and a long red measuring tape. Carlos and Jane watched in amazement as Evie set down the bag of shoes and leaned out the window again. She maneuvered the measuring tape around, measuring different angles and distances on the roof. She wrote everything down in a little notebook she'd pulled out of her shoe bag. Carlos tried to make sense of what she was writing, but it was a bunch of mathematical scribbles he didn't understand. Evie had always been way better at math than Carlos.

"Uh, Evie," he said. "What are you doing?"

But Evie didn't answer; she just continued to work quickly and quietly, measuring and writing, writing and measuring. Occasionally she paused long enough to tap her forehead with her pencil before scribbling something else down. Then, after she was done with the roof, she started to pull shoes out of her giant bag and measure those, too. Carlos noticed that all the pairs had ridiculously high heels on them. Some looked to be at least five inches tall.

"How do girls walk in those?" he whispered to Jane.

"Very carefully," Jane whispered back. It was as though neither of them wanted to speak too loudly, for fear of interrupting Evie during her . . . well, whatever it was she was doing. Carlos continued to check the clock on his phone, his anxiety rising a notch with every minute that passed. He was tempted to tell Evie to forget it. They should move on and find something else on the list to tackle.

But he knew he had to trust her. Even though Carlos had no idea what Evie was doing, *she* certainly seemed to. So he sat back and let her work. Finally, after what felt like hours had passed, Evie looked up from her notepad. She was surrounded by several pairs of shoes. "Aha! I've got it!"

Carlos waited for her to say more, and when she didn't, he asked, "You've got what?"

Evie picked up a pair of shoes from the pile next to her. They had wedge heels that were so high they reminded Carlos of castle walls. Evie held them proudly above her head. "I figured out how to get that blasted piece of fruit."

SIT, STAY, HIGH HEEL

This girl has taken fashionably
fierce to a new level.

"This is making me very nervous," Jane squeaked as she and Carlos watched Evie through the open window. She had the high wedge shoes strapped onto her feet and was walking very slowly across the roof.

"Don't worry!" Evie called back. "I got this."

And it was true. She evidently *did* have this. She had somehow calculated the slope of the roof and the height and angle of the wedge shoes so that they counteracted each other. And she'd done such a precise job that she was literally standing straight up. She wasn't slanted at all. The shoes and the roof were a perfect mathematical match.

"How are you not terrified right now?" Jane called out to Evie, grabbing Carlos's hand and squeezing it.

"I'm from the Isle," Evie said, as though this explained everything. But it didn't for Carlos. He was from the Isle, too, and there was *no way* anyone could convince him to walk out on the roof wearing shoes like that. But that's why Evie was a rock star. Nothing seemed to scare her. She was always up for whatever scheme anyone had in mind . . . including her own.

Carlos held his breath as Evie scurried to the edge of the roof and grabbed on to the top of the hazelberry tree. With one hand supporting her weight on the trunk of the tree, she leaned forward, and with the other hand, reached toward the nearest hanging bunch of hazelberry. But she couldn't seem to reach, so she took another step toward the edge of the roof.

And that's when one of her ankles twisted at a strange angle and Evie started to fall forward.

Evie screamed.

Jane screamed.

Even Carlos screamed.

Evie caught the tree trunk with her free hand, stopping herself from tumbling over the edge of the building. She was now positioned at a terrifying angle, her feet standing unsteadily on the roof, her body completely horizontal, suspended over the ground, and her hands clutching the trunk of the tree. If her grip were to give out or her feet were to slip, she would most certainly fall.

Gulping, Carlos glanced at the ground below. It was so far. He squeezed Jane's hand back.

"Don't worry!" Evie called out again. "I still got this!"

But now Carlos wasn't so sure if that was true. "Just come back inside!" he called back to her.

But Evie didn't seem to want to listen. Carlos watched her shuffle her feet closer to the edge of the roof and lean even farther forward toward the tree. Then she stretched one hand out and reached for the hazelberry.

"What is she doing?" Jane whispered anxiously to Carlos.

"I think she's still going for the fruit!"

"Oh, gosh, no!" Jane exclaimed.

"Evie!" Carlos called out. "Just leave it! It's not worth it!"

But Evie was ignoring her team captain again. And in that moment, Carlos realized it wasn't because he was a bad leader. Evie was just a *very* bad follower. The girl operated entirely on her own.

Carlos watched, paralyzed, from the window as Evie's grasp finally hooked around the hazelberry and she gave it a yank. The fruit came free, but the jerking motion seemed to throw Evie off-balance. She swayed a bit and Jane sucked in her breath.

But Evie was quickly able to right herself. She slowly brought her hand to her pocket and placed the hazelberry inside.

"How on earth is she going to get back now?" Jane asked Carlos, but Carlos just shook his head. He had *no* idea. He just hoped *Evie* knew the answer to that question.

And, apparently, she did. She placed both hands back on the bark of the tree, and with a grunt and a heave, pushed hard against the tree trunk.

In the next instant, time stood still. Carlos fought the urge to close his eyes. For a moment, Evie seemed to be suspended in midair, as though she were flying high above the ground.

"I can't look!" Jane said, turning to bury her head in Carlos's shoulder. Carlos gently rubbed her back, trying to soothe her fears. But he could do nothing to calm his own fears. If Evie fell, he'd never forgive himself.

Carlos heard a crash, and he blinked and focused back on the roof. Evie had managed to push herself all the way back until she was sitting on the slanted roof.

She tried to stand up, but her ankle must have

been hurting from the strange twist. She quickly lost her balance and sat back down.

She's not going to make it back here, Carlos thought with dread. *She's going to be stuck out on that roof.* They'd have to tell Fairy Godmother. Fairy Godmother would have to send a helicopter or something to help pull her inside.

Pull her inside.

The words bounced around in Carlos's brain before finally settling down somewhere they made sense.

"That's it!" he shouted, startling Jane. "Evie, stay right there!"

He backed away from her and ran over to his bed. He pulled all the blankets and sheets off and began to tie the ends of them together.

"What are you doing?" Jane asked.

"I'm making sure my best friend doesn't fall off that roof," Carlos said.

Jane's gaze fell to the makeshift rope Carlos was constructing and her eyes lit up with recognition. "Oh! Of course! I'll help." She ran to Jay's bed and stripped his sheets, tying the ends together, creating her own rope. Then she found the end of Carlos's rope and joined the two together with a tight knot.

Carlos dragged the giant rope toward the window and flung it outside. The end landed close enough for Evie to reach. "Grab hold!" Carlos commanded, and thankfully, this time Evie obeyed.

She clutched the end of the rope and Carlos and Jane heaved and heaved, looking like sailors pulling an anchor from the water. Finally, Evie made it to the window and collapsed back inside the dorm room.

She lay on the floor for a long moment, trying to catch her breath and composure. Then she sat up and pulled the hazelberry from her pocket. "I think this item needs to be worth two *thousand* points."

And Carlos, Evie, and Jane all burst into laughter.

DIGGING UP
THE TRUTH

It's down to the wire. We
really need a miracle.

There were now exactly thirteen minutes left until
the annual Auradon Prep Scavenger Hunt ended.
Evie and Jane peered over Carlos's shoulder, looking at the list on his phone.

"It's a lost cause," Carlos said with a sigh.
"With the wooden puppet, the glass slipper, and
the hazelberry, we only have thirty-five points. I
know for a fact that Jay's team has at least fifty-five,
probably more. So unless one of us can figure out
what a violet-gold pixie fork is and how to get one

in the next thirteen minutes, we're going to lose."

He shut off the screen of his phone and returned it to his pocket. Then he turned to his team. "I'm sorry to let you all down," he said, lowering his head. "But I don't think there's a stone with our names on it this year."

Evie rushed forward to comfort Carlos. "Hey, it's okay. We did our best. That's all that matters."

Carlos dug the toe of his shoe into the carpet. He knew Evie was right. It didn't matter if they won or lost; what mattered was that they had worked hard and stuck together as a team. But still, Carlos really wanted to win this.

"I wonder what a violet-gold pixie fork is anyway," Carlos muttered. "I can't find it anywhere online. Fairy Godmother probably put it on the list as a distraction. It probably doesn't even exist."

"It exists." Jane's voice was soft and tentative, and Carlos and Evie both swung their gazes toward their friend who, up until that moment, had been suspiciously quiet.

"What?" Carlos asked.

Jane looked at her feet. "Fairies use them at weddings. They're a very special utensil used for very special occasions."

"How do you know that?" Evie asked, stepping toward Jane.

Jane still refused to look either of them in the eye. "Because Carina Potts has a jarful of them in her supply closet. I had to inventory the whole thing last summer. I counted them one by one." She let out a sad chuckle. "Which was hard because they're very tiny."

Carlos was shocked. "You mean you knew where to find one all of this time and you didn't say anything?"

Jane's eyes filled with tears. "Only because I knew it was a lost cause. Carina Potts doesn't like me. Plus, she's probably too busy and important to take my calls anyway."

"Jane," Evie began tenderly. "That can't be true. I can't imagine anyone *not* liking you."

"Well, she doesn't," Jane said somewhat bitterly. "I worked so hard for her and she never even paid me a single compliment. She never even said thank you!"

All that time, Carlos had remained silent. Jane must have thought he was mad at her for keeping the secret, because she said, "I'm sorry, Carlos. I'm really sorry."

But Carlos wasn't mad. At least not at Jane. He was, however, furious at Carina Potts. How dare she make Jane feel that way! Jane was the sweetest, most hardworking person Carlos knew. And if Carina Potts was too blind to see that, then Carlos would *make* her see that.

"Where is her office?" Carlos said. His voice was calm. Controlled. Despite the frustration that was boiling up inside him.

"Carlos," Jane protested, "it's not worth it. We don't have much time left now. There's no way you're going to be able to—"

"Where is it?" Carlos insisted.

Jane surrendered with a sigh. "It's downtown. But it's not worth even—"

Carlos didn't allow Jane to finish. He was

already out the door. He was already running down the hallway. He could hear Jane calling out behind him, telling him to stop. But he wouldn't stop. Jane was his friend. His *teammate*. Carlos was her captain. And Fairy Godmother was right. A leader protects his team.

BAD TO THE BONE

I'm feeling riled up, but I'm gonna
play it cool. I'm gonna be composed.
I'm gonna tell Carina Potts exactly
what's on my mind. But I'm not
going to lose my temper.

When Carlos arrived at the Potts Parties office in
downtown Auradon, he had already worked out
what he was going to say. He refused to handle
things the way his mother handled things. He
refused to shout and rant and throw his arms in
the air. He would be calm, but firm.

Jane and Evie arrived a few moments after

him, breathless from trying to keep up. "Carlos, please don't do this," Jane said. "It's not worth even trying to talk to her."

"She owes you a favor," Carlos said simply. Then he marched right into the building, right past the receptionist at the front desk who tried to stop him, and right into Carina Potts's office.

Carina was a thin, stern-looking woman with white-blond hair and icy blue eyes. She didn't smile when Carlos barged in. She just peered at him over the top of her red-rimmed glasses and said in a sharp voice, "Yes? Can I help you?"

Carlos stood up taller and pushed his shoulders back. He'd never felt more like a leader than he did at this moment. "I'm friends with Jane. Your intern from last summer."

Carina opened her mouth to speak, but Carlos cut her off with a raise of his hand and said, "I'll be the one speaking, thank you."

Carina fell silent, looking slightly baffled.

"Regardless of what you think of Jane, she worked hard for you. You will most likely never hire an intern as dedicated, organized, and effi-cient as Jane. I don't know why you never paid her a single compliment. Maybe you just fail to recognize talent when you see it, but I don't. I recognize it. Jane is one of the most talented people I've ever met. And if you can't see that, then it's *your* loss. Not hers."

Carina stared blankly at Carlos, as though he were speaking a foreign language. Carlos glanced behind him, looking for Jane, but he didn't see her anywhere. He wondered if she had lost her nerve and stayed out in the lobby.

"I don't know what you're talking about," Carina responded flatly a moment later.

Carlos's mouth fell open. He reminded himself to stay collected. Stay cool. "I'm talking about your intern from last summer. I can't believe you don't even remember—"

"Of course, I remember *Jane*," Carina said, shaking her head. "What I mean is, I don't know what you're talking about when you accuse me of not recognizing talent. Jane was hands-down the best intern I've ever had." Then Carina's voice softened and she removed her glasses. "I'm sorry about the compliment thing. Sometimes I get so busy, I forget to tell people what an excellent job they're doing. It's something I'm working on. If you see Jane, would you please tell her how much I appreciate her? And if she's ever interested in interning for me again, I would hire her in a heartbeat."

Carlos was so shocked by Carina's unexpected response that he just stood there, speechless, staring at her for a long time.

Then a tiny faraway voice said, "I would love to intern for you again."

Carlos and Carina both startled, and Carlos turned around to see Jane walking through the door. She must have been hiding just outside, listening.

Carina smiled, revealing perfect white teeth. "Jane! It's so good to see you again. I've missed you. My supply closet has fallen into complete disarray since you left."

Jane cracked a small smile. "I'd be happy to come organize it for you anytime."

Carlos glanced at the clock on his phone. *Three* minutes until the hunt was over.

"Um, Jane," he said, gesturing to the time.

Jane nodded, clearing her throat. When she spoke again, she sounded confident and self-assured. Nothing like the girl she'd been only a few minutes before. "Carina," she said, "would it be possible to ask you for a small favor?"

Carina's blue eyes sparkled and Carlos's hopes soared up to the roof. "Anything for you, Jane."

LICKETY-SPLIT

*Phew! We made it back in the nick
of time. Just as the buzzer rang!*

The entire student body of Auradon Prep was
assembled in the banquet hall. Everyone was chattering animatedly about the hunt. About the points
they'd scored, which item had been the hardest to
acquire, and which had been the easiest.

Carlos and his team had just managed to snap
the photograph of the violet-gold pixie fork in
Carina's supply closet before racing back to the
school.

They collapsed into chairs at one of the dining

tables and Carlos let out a sigh of relief. They'd made it. They'd ended the hunt with a whopping sixty points, which Carlos thought was quite a feat, given that for the majority of the day they'd only had ten.

"All right, everyone!" Fairy Godmother announced, holding her hands in the air to gather the students' attention. "Settle down. Settle down. I trust you all had an action-packed scavenger hunt today. Let's tally up the points and see who has won. If you would kindly send your photos to the school server now."

Carlos flipped through the photos on his phone, quickly selecting the ones that documented their points—the wooden puppet, the glass slipper, the hazelberry, and the violet-gold pixie fork—and clicking the button to upload them to the Auradon Prep server. As the photos zoomed off, Carlos smiled. He was happy with the way the day had turned out. He felt accomplished. Carlos had no idea if sixty points was enough to win, but he was proud of those sixty points anyway.

"Okay!" Fairy Godmother said about five minutes later, after the photos from all the teams had been uploaded. She glanced at the screen of her tablet. "It looks like we had a close hunt this year, but I have the top three teams here, ready to be announced." Fairy Godmother cleared her throat dramatically and peered at her tablet. "In third place . . . is Jordan, Ben, and Chad, with sixty-five points!"

Carlos's heart immediately sunk.

Sixty-five points.

They hadn't even made it into the top three. Carlos's team only had sixty points. Jane and Evie immediately tried to make him feel better. "I'm sorry, Carlos," Jane said, rubbing his shoulder. "It just wasn't our year."

"Yeah," Evie added, putting her arm around Carlos and giving him a squeeze. "There's always next year."

Carlos laughed at their efforts. "You guys. I'm fine. Seriously. I had fun today."

And it was the truth. He *did* have fun. And

he *was* fine. Sure, he would have liked to win. He would have liked to make it into the top three. But in the end, it didn't matter. He'd found the leader in himself and that was enough.

Jordan, Ben, and Chad hurried to the front of the banquet hall to accept their award—a blue-and-gold ribbon commemorating their achievement. As the crowd cheered and Jordan bowed and basked in the attention, Carlos pulled out his phone again and flipped through the photos from the day, remembering all of the moments his team had shared.

There were the five photos of them unsuccessfully attempting to capture their pose in the window of Belle's Boutique. Three of Carlos dragging Evie into the window while Evie typed into her phone, and two of Jane mid-sneeze. He chuckled at the memory. Even thought he was bummed they never got one of all three of them together in the window, at least he could laugh at how silly the pictures were.

Then there was the photo of Carlos and Henry,

the boy they'd found crying in the train station and helped reunite with his mother. In that picture, Henry was grinning up at the camera in his Carlos-style pants and adorable oversized RAD REP T-shirt. He really did look like he'd just met a celebrity.

"And in second place," Fairy Godmother announced, causing Carlos to look up, "is Jay, Mal, and Lonnie, with seventy points!"

Seventy points!

They'd only lost to Jay's team by ten points! Carlos felt a squeeze in his chest as he glanced from Jay and his team to the photo of Henry on his phone. That Auradon Express ticket was worth twenty points, which meant if they hadn't stopped to help Henry find his mother, they would have ended the game with eighty points and they might have won.

"And in first place, with seventy-five points . . ." Fairy Godmother said theatrically.

Carlos sighed. They definitely would have

won. They would have had eighty points. The first place team got seventy-five! He continued to stare down at the picture. At the huge grin on Henry's face. He supposed it was all worth it. Carlos may not have been a hero in the annual Auradon Prep Scavenger Hunt, but he was a hero in the eyes of this boy. Henry looked so happy to be standing next to Carlos.

"Carlos, Jane, and Evie!" a voice said, and suddenly, the room erupted in applause. For a moment, Carlos didn't know what was happening. Why had that voice said their names? Why was everyone turning to him and clapping? Why was Jane jumping up and down?

"We won!" Jane exclaimed. "We did it!"

Carlos shook his head. There must have been some kind of mistake. They hadn't won. They hadn't collected seventy-five points; they'd only collected sixty. Had there been a miscalculation? Had Fairy Godmother accidentally counted those items Carlos had collected using the dog collar?

But that seemed impossible. He'd deleted those photos from his phone. There was no evidence of them.

"Carlos?" Jane said. Carlos blinked and tried to focus on her face. But it was too hard with all the yelling and clapping.

"I have to tell her," he said dazedly, pushing his way to the front of the room, "There's been a mistake. I have to tell her."

But before he could reach the headmistress, Fairy Godmother went on. "And the items that nabbed the win for Carlos's team were . . ."

Carlos stopped and listened curiously.

"The violet-gold pixie fork for twenty-five points, the hazelberry for twenty-five points, the puppet made of wood for five points, the slipper made of glass for five points, and the Auradon Prep gym T-shirt from at least twenty years ago for fifteen points, making a total of seventy-five points!"

Carlos gaped at Fairy Godmother. Something was wrong. She'd made a mistake. They didn't get the old gym T-shirt. They'd never even *tried* to get that one. He pulled out his phone and stared at the pictures again. And that's when he noticed something unusual. Along with the other photos, Carlos had accidentally uploaded the picture of Henry and him to the Auradon Prep server. His finger must have accidentally clicked it in his haste to select all the photos.

But that still didn't make any sense. It wasn't a picture of an old Auradon Prep gym T-shirt. It was a picture of Carlos and a random kid at the train station.

Carlos's thoughts stopped short as he stared at the picture on his phone. With his thumb and forefinger, he pinched the screen, zooming all the way in on Henry's shirt.

RAD REP

Carlos had assumed it was some kind of band. But now, as he zoomed in farther, he could see that there were more letters. Or rather, there were empty spaces where letters *used* to be. Like they'd been worn off over the years. Like the shirt was . . .

Old.

If he squinted, he could almost see the faded outlines of the letters that had worn off.

AURADON PREP

Carlos suddenly remembered something the boy had said to him after they'd found him on the platform. "My daddy went to Auradon Prep a long time ago. I can't wait until I can go."

The shirt! It belonged to Henry's father. That's why it was so big on him!

They'd found an old Auradon Prep gym T-shirt! They just hadn't known they'd found one! Which meant, Carlos realized with delight, that helping that boy hadn't *cost* them the hunt, it had *won* them the hunt!

LEADER OF
THE PACK

Turns out I didn't need that old
dog collar after all. We won, and
I proved I had what it takes to
be a leader. But I couldn't have
done it without my team.

The sun was shining. The sky was blue. The sound
of trumpets and drums could be heard from miles
away. Fairy Godmother said the magic word and
two hundred colorful balloons were released into
the air, flying higher and higher until they were
nothing but specks of confetti in the sky.

Carlos followed them with his eyes before

turning back to the courtyard, where the whole school had gathered for the celebration.

It was finally the big day of the stone unveiling ceremony.

The names Carlos, Jane, and Evie had been carved into one of the giant diamond-shaped paving stones in the courtyard, and now it was going to be unveiled. Carlos had been waiting for this moment for over a week. Ever since Fairy Godmother had called their names at the end of the annual Auradon Prep Scavenger Hunt. He still couldn't believe they had pulled off that win. It felt like a dream to him. A wonderful fairy tale dream.

Carlos supposed that's what life in Auradon was all about. There were no screaming mothers or scary back alleys you had to run through to get home. This really was the place where dreams came true. Carlos's certainly had. He'd finally proved to everyone that he had what it took to lead a team to victory. But most of all, he'd proved it to himself. He'd always known he was meant for great things, but there had still been that voice in the back of his mind—the voice of his mother—telling him he couldn't do it. It wasn't possible. He'd always be a sidekick, never a hero. And without even knowing he had done it, he'd listened to that voice. He'd trusted it. It's what had led him to use the dog collar in the first place, instead of just trusting himself and his teammates. Carlos would still be the nice guy who his friends looked to for help. And that was fine. More than fine. That was great. But it didn't mean Carlos couldn't *also* be the guy his friends looked to for leadership. In fact, Carlos had learned that maybe the two things were related.

"And now," Fairy Godmother began in a regal, ceremonial tone, "we are pleased to unveil the stone commemorating the champions of this year's Auradon Prep Scavenger Hunt!" She gave the signal and the sheet that covered the stone was lifted gracefully from the ground.

Carlos held his breath. Of course, he knew exactly what the engraving would say, but he was still so anxious to see it. And, of course, to see the reactions on Jane's and Evie's faces when they saw what he had done. They had no idea what was coming.

The veil was lifted. The stone was made visible to all. And everyone in the courtyard let out a simultaneous gasp of surprise. They'd never seen anything like it. And that's because it was the first of its kind. While all the other stones in the courtyard listed a team captain (marked with the initials TC), and two team members (marked with the initials TM), Carlos had told Fairy Godmother that he wanted something different.

He stared down at the stone and smiled contentedly to himself. Different was definitely what he got. The stone read:

CARLOS

JANE

EVIE

"What did you do?" Jane asked. She looked both delighted and confused at the same time.

Carlos shrugged, playing innocent. "I had them carve our names into the stone."

Evie shook her head. "I don't get it. Where are the titles? Team captain and team members?"

Carlos stood between his teammates and put an arm around each of their shoulders. "The titles don't matter. We worked hard. *All* of us. And we won. Together." He looked to Evie, then to Jane. And he smiled the smile of a champion. "The rest is just details."